T MW01032180

BASIL FREDERICK ALBERT COPPER was born in London in 1923. As a boy, Copper moved with his family to Kent, where he attended the local grammar school and developed an early taste for the works of M.R. James and Edgar Allan Poe. In his teens he began training as an apprentice journalist, but with the outbreak of the Second World War, he found himself put in charge of a local newspaper office while also serving in the Home Guard. He then joined the Royal Navy and served as a radio operator with a gunboat flotilla off the Normandy beaches during the D-Day operations.

After the war, Copper resumed his career in journalism. He made his fiction debut in *The Fifth Book of Pan Horror Stories* (1964) with "The Spider," for which he was paid £10. His first novel, a tongue-in-cheek crime story in the Dashiell Hammett/Raymond Chandler mode, *The Dark Mirror*, was turned down by 32 publishers because it was too long, before Robert Hale eventually published a cut-down version. Four years later, in 1970, Copper gave up journalism to write full-time.

Copper published some fifty novels featuring the Los Angeles private detective Mike Faraday and also wrote several horror and supernatural novels and a number of collections of macabre short stories. His horror fiction in particular has been receiving renewed attention recently with new editions from PS Publishing and Valancourt Books. Basil Copper died at age 89 in 2013 after suffering from Alzheimer's disease.

STEPHEN JONES is a prolific editor of horror anthologies, including PS Publishing's two-volume *Darkness, Mist & Shadow: The Collected Macabre Tales of Basil Copper* (2010) and the author of *Basil Copper: A Life in Books* (2008), which won the British Fantasy Award. His books have previously received the Hugo Award, several Bram Stoker Awards, and the World Fantasy Award.

ALSO BY BASIL COPPER

Not After Nightfall: Stories of the Strange and Terrible (1967)
From Evil's Pillow (1973)
The Great White Space (1974)*
When Footsteps Echo: Tales of Terror and the Unknown (1975)
The Curse of the Fleers (1976)
And Afterward, the Dark: Seven Tales (1977)
Here Be Daemons: Tales of Horror and the Uneasy (1978)
Necropolis (1980)*
Voices of Doom: Tales of Terror and the Uncanny (1980)
Into the Silence (1983)
The House of the Wolf (1983)
The Black Death (1991)
Whispers in the Night: Stories of the Mysterious & Macabre (1999)
Cold Hand on My Shoulder: Tales of Terror and Suspense (2002)
Knife in the Back: Tales of Twilight and Torment (2005)
Darkness, Mist and Shadow: The Collected Macabre Tales (2010, 2 vols.)

* Available from Valancourt Books

THE GREAT WHITE SPACE

by

BASIL COPPER

With a new introduction by
STEPHEN JONES

𝕶𝖆𝖓𝖘𝖆𝖘 𝕮𝖎𝖙𝖞:
VALANCOURT BOOKS
2013

The Great White Space by Basil Copper
First published London: Robert Hale, 1974
First Valancourt Books edition 2013

Copyright © 1974 by Basil Copper
Introduction © 2013 by Stephen Jones

Published by Valancourt Books, Kansas City, Missouri
Publisher & Editor: JAMES D. JENKINS
20th Century Series Editor: SIMON STERN, University of Toronto
http://www.valancourtbooks.com

All rights reserved. The use of any part of this publication
reproduced, transmitted in any form or by any means, electronic,
mechanical, photocopying, recording, or otherwise, or stored
in a retrieval system, without prior written consent of the
publisher, constitutes an infringement of the copyright law.

Library of Congress Cataloging-in-Publication Data

Copper, Basil.
The great white space / by Basil Copper ; with a new introduction
by Stephen Jones – First Valancourt Books edition.
pages ; cm. – (20th century series)
ISBN 978-1-939140-38-8 *(acid free paper)*
I. Title.
PR6053.0658G74 2013
823'.914–dc23

2013009344

All Valancourt Books publications are printed on acid free paper
that meets all ANSI standards for archival quality paper.

Cover art by Eric Robertson
Set in Dante MT 11/13.5

INTRODUCTION

ALTHOUGH BEST KNOWN as an author of macabre short stories and Lovecraftian novels, Basil Copper was also the author of two popular detective series, set almost half-a-century and two totally different genres apart.

Born in London on February 5, 1924, Basil Copper soon moved with his family to Kent. "Little Willy", as he was affectionately known, attended The Tonbridge Senior Boys School, where he contributed early fiction to the school magazine, took part in amateur dramatics, and was a member of The Leicester Football eleven.

When grammar school failed to satisfy his wide range of interests, Copper started haunting the local bookshops and libraries. A voracious reader, he soon discovered the works of Algernon Blackwood, M.R. James and Edgar Allan Poe, whose influence was to serve him well in later years.

While attending a local commercial college, he learned bookkeeping, economics and the useful skills of shorthand and touch-typing, which proved invaluable when he began training as an apprentice journalist. With the outbreak of World War II seeing so many reporters conscripted, Copper soon found himself in charge of a county newspaper branch office at the age of seventeen, while also serving in the Home Guard.

He then joined the Royal Navy, in which he served for four years in Light Coastal Forces in Newhaven, Portsmouth and Portland. Having completed a course at the Glasgow Wireless College, he mostly served on gunboats and torpedo boats, and he was a radio operator on board a motor gunboat flotilla off the Normandy beaches during the D-Day operations. While escorting the first wave of landing craft ashore, Copper's flotilla lost half its six craft, mostly to acoustic mines.

After going on survivor's leave, he subsequently spent two years on radio stations in Egypt, Malta and Gibraltar, before demobilization. Having contributed pieces to the London *Times* since the outbreak of the war, Copper resumed his career in the provincial press, working for the *Sevenoaks News* and the *Kent and Sussex Cou-*

rier before rising to editor of the Sevenoaks edition of the *Kent Messenger*. He also contributed to three national newspapers: the *London Evening Standard*, the *Evening News* and *The Star*.

Basil Copper made his debut as a fiction writer with "The Spider" in *The Fifth Book of Pan Horror Stories* (1964), for which he was paid the princely sum of £10 by the editor, Herbert van Thal. Around the same time, he began writing his first novel while working in the newspaper office. He set out to write a tongue-in-cheek crime story in the Dashiell Hammett/Raymond Chandler mode entitled *The Dark Mirror*. When it was completed, he sent it to thirty-two publishers, who all turned it down because it was too long. After he made four attempts to cut it down, Robert Hale eventually published the novel in 1966. His writing career took off, and four years later he gave up journalism to write full-time.

The Dark Mirror launched a series of hard-boiled thrillers featuring Los Angeles private investigator Mike Faraday, an obvious and acknowledged homage to Chandler's Philip Marlowe. Although critics admired the author's authentic descriptions of the City of Angels, Copper had in fact never been to California. All his knowledge was gleaned from watching old movies and referring to maps. The first book was popular enough to spawn a series and, over the next twenty-two years Copper produced fifty-two volumes, often at the rate of two or more books a year, until the series ended in 1988. Faraday's charm as a tough protagonist and poetry-quoting narrator, ably supported by his faithful secretary Stella, proved popular with readers in other countries as well, and the books were translated into numerous foreign-language editions.

American author August Derleth had begun writing his series of stories about consulting detective Solar Pons (whose name in Latin literally means "Bridge of Light") in the late 1920s after he received a letter from Sir Arthur Conan Doyle stating that there would be no further tales of Sherlock Holmes. Derleth's Pons was closely modelled on Doyle's character—he lived at 7B Praed Street, not far from Paddington Station; his own Watson was Dr Lyndon Parker, and Mrs Johnson was their long-suffering landlady. Eight volumes of these Holmes pastiches were published between 1945 and 1973 under Derleth's specialist Mycroft & Moran imprint.

Unfortunately, the author's research left much to be desired, and seven years after Derleth's death in 1973 Copper was controversially asked to revise and edit the entire series of seventy short stories and one novel. The task took almost eighteen months, and the result was published by Mycroft & Moran as *The Solar Pons Omnibus* in 1982. Copper was invited to continue the Pontine canon himself, and he produced seven collections of novellas and the novel *Solar Pons versus the Devil's Claw* (2004). Copper's Pons stories have been collected by various publishers, although the author has disowned some editions after unauthorized rewriting by in-house editors.

The first of his macabre and supernatural novels (like the actor Boris Karloff, he disliked the term "horror") was the transgressive *The Great White Space*, originally published in 1974 by Robert Hale & Company in the United Kingdom and the following year by St. Martin's Press in America.

Although the dedication to "Howard Phillips Lovecraft and August Derleth – Openers of the Way" immediately establishes the book to be in the 1930s pulp tradition of those authors' "Cthulhu Mythos", the narrative owes just as much to the works of Jules Verne and Sir Arthur Conan Doyle as larger-than-life Professor Clark Ashton Scarsdale (obviously inspired by Doyle's Professor Challenger and named after pulp writer Clark Ashton Smith) leads the Great Northern Expedition through vast subterranean tunnels into the center of the Earth.

Their ill-fated tractor journey takes them beyond "The Plain of Darkness" to an underground lake, a sinister embalming gallery and a secret underground city, before they reach the ultimate horror that awaits them – the Great White Space itself.

The book was reissued in paperback by Manor Books in 1976, and in Britain by Sphere Books four years later. "This paperback edition gave away the secret of the final line in the cover illustration!" the author later complained. Except for a German translation in 2002, this was the last time the novel saw print until now.

Following on from *The Great White Space*, the author's other novels included a companion piece, *Into the Silence* (1983), and *The Black Death* (1991), along with a trio of Gothics comprising *The Curse of the Fleers* (1976), *Necropolis* (1980) and *The House of the Wolf* (1983), the latter two titles published by August Derleth's legendary Arkham House imprint.

Two of Copper's early collections of short stories, *From Evil's Pillow* (1973) and *And Afterward, the Dark: Seven Tales* (1977), were also issued by Arkham, and his shorter work was also collected in *Not After Nightfall: Stories of the Strange and the Terrible* (1967), *When Footsteps Echo: Tales of Terror and the Unknown* (1975), *Here Be Daemons: Tales of Horror and the Uneasy* (1978), *Voices of Doom: Tales of Terror and the Uncanny* (1980), *Whispers in the Night: Stories of the Mysterious and the Macabre* (1999), *Cold Hand on My Shoulder: Tales of Terror & Suspense* (2002), and the self-published *Knife in the Back: Tales of Twilight and Torment* (2005).

In recent years there has been a resurgence of interest in Copper's work, starting with my own British Fantasy Award-winning bio/bibliography *Basil Copper: A Life in Books* (2008) from PS Publishing, who went on to collect all the author's macabre fiction in the impressive two-volume set *Darkness, Mist & Shadow* (2010) and reissued his 1976 novel *The Curse of the Fleers* in a restored version for the first time in 2012.

Now Valancourt Books has published long-overdue reissues of *The Great White Space* and *Necropolis*, and forthcoming from PS is a complete collection of all the author's Solar Pons tales.

Copper's story "Camera Obscura" was dramatized on the TV series *Rod Serling's Night Gallery* in 1971 starring René Auberjonois and Ross Martin, while the author's *conte cruel* "The Recompensing of Albano Pizar" was adapted as "Invitation to the Vaults" for BBC Radio 4 in 1991.

A member of the Crime Writers' Association for more than thirty years, serving as its Chairman from 1981-82 and on its committee for seven years, he was elected a Knight of Mark Twain in 1979 by the Mark Twain Society of America for his outstanding "contribution to modern fiction", while the Praed Street Irregulars twice honored him for his Solar Pons series. In 2010, the World Horror Convention presented him with its inaugural Lifetime Achievement Award.

Basil Copper died on April 3, 2013, aged 89. He had been suffering from Alzheimer's disease for a couple of years.

STEPHEN JONES

April 14, 2013

THE GREAT WHITE SPACE

For
Howard Phillips Lovecraft
and
August Derleth
Openers of the Way

One

I

There are those – and they have been many – who were inclined to dismiss my theories as the ramblings of a man in fever. Certainly, the circumstances surrounding the Great Northern Expedition were such as to drive a sensitive person into mindless idiocy. The shifting lights in the sky which preceded the Coming in the spring of 1932 passed generally unnoticed by the world's press, but the disappearance of so distinguished a field worker as Professor Clark Ashton Scarsdale into the blank void of those vast, unknowable spaces, could hardly fail to arouse comment.

And I, the solitary survivor of the penetration made by the small group of five, have seen enough, God knows, to make the strongest man unhinged. And so I must live on, my story unbelieved, and scorned, until such time as the truth emerges. The world may indeed fear if that period should ever come. Meanwhile I continue the only man on earth who knows why and how poor Scarsdale went into the Great White Space, never to be seen again by mortal men. But what gibbering, formless things he may now dwell with apart from the world – it is this and other knowledge, long pent within my overheated brain, which makes me start at shadows; or awake fearfully at the night wind's insidious tapping at my bedroom blinds.

It is the wind itself which makes me abhor the winter in these latitudes; keening from off the world's dreariest places it seems to freeze the very heart. Robson, my old friend, and the one most inclined to place some small faith in my theories, has truly described me as "a man without a shadow". He meant only that my emaciated form and spectral aspect were hardly substantial enough to imprint their own image on the ground; to me the phrase suggests awful things and in particular that dreadful day in which the Great White Space first came within the knowledge of living men.

In setting down these sketchy notes before the events which they describe have irrevocably burned themselves into insanity within my mind, I do not expect to be believed. At best they will confirm the prejudiced in their bigotry; at worst, if discovered untimely, they will undoubtedly lead to my speedy committal to some secluded asylum where I shall assuredly end my days. That these are numbered I have no doubt; yet even the relief of oblivion is denied me for may I not, beyond the wall of the thin veil that men call life, meet those Others who gyrate and ponderously undulate far out in the utmost reaches of space?

And to be brought face to face with the thing that once was Scarsdale, is a fear too frightful to be contemplated; an eternity in such company and the terror of other beings which are such blasphemies that even I dare not hint at, makes me cling to such poor life as I have. I can still sleep occasionally without dreaming, thank God; this at least is something. And the notes, if they serve the small purpose of warning one sensitive person of the dangers overshadowing the earth, may yet spell great goodness for mankind.

But where to begin? This is indeed the first of my problems, lest my sanity be mocked at the outset. I was born then, Frederick Seddon Plowright; such life as I enjoyed until attaining my majority is no concern of this narrative, still less of interest to the general reader. After graduation I studied various outré subjects on the fringe of my scientific knowledge and eventually drifted into photography. I became an excellent portrayer of scientific and geographic subjects and accompanied a number of important expeditions earlier in the century, notably von Hagenbeck's penetration of the Quartz Mountains of Outer Mongolia; and of Francis Luttrell's major earth-boring investigations in the Nevada Desert of 1929, an adventure which almost cost me my life.

My films, depicting as they did, fantastic and extraordinary landscapes and animals at the ends of the earth attracted much attention not only in scientific and geographic journals but in the popular press so that I began to find my services in greater demand. I was living comfortably and as I had the sagacity to secure all the copyrights to my negatives I found in my mid-thirties that I had more than enough money for my needs. So I began to choose my assignments with more care, selecting only those which promised adventurous and even bizarre circumstances in their commission. It was in 1931 that I first heard the name of Clark Ashton Scarsdale. It was, I believe, in connection with the great sledge journey made in the Antarctic by the late Crosby Patterson; the cruel and tragic fate of Patterson and his five companions is too well-known to bear repetition, but Scarsdale had been consulted on certain aspects of their end. His opinions were widely reported in the press and I remember vividly one photograph, which depicted a strong, bearded figure, examining some of the curious rock inscriptions which had been found at the spot where the six Polar explorers had met death in a most terrible form.

A year or two after this I was myself commissioned to photograph the inscriptions by the Board of Trustees of the Chicago Museum which had originally financed Patterson's great journey; this was a fascinating task and took me upwards of three weeks, though the inscriptions and their background are not relevant to this narrative. I later applied to and was given permission by the Trustees to publish a number of the photographs in Geographica, a learned magazine in which the increasing bulk of my work was to appear.

This material itself was the cause of further publicity and it was some two months following the publication of the Geographica pictures that I received the first of several enigmatic letters from Professor Scarsdale. But the preliminary contact with a being who was to have such a profound effect upon my life, was prosaic in the extreme. He merely offered congratulations on the technicalities involved in securing such original photographs and commented that they had been extremely helpful to him in his investigations.

He did not at that time suggest a meeting and I should no doubt have soon forgotten this fleeting correspondence had I not, in replying to him, sent him a complete set of prints I had taken for the Museum. These, of course, were greater in number than those which had appeared in the public press and the detail into which I had gone in the matter of enlarging certain portions of the diagrams and hieroglyphs caused the Professor considerable excitement. I shortly received a letter couched in extremely cordial terms and suggesting a meeting at some time and place mutually convenient.

2

I was living in London at the time and the Professor's letter was written from an address in Surrey so there was no great difficulty in arranging to meet; my first view of Scarsdale in the flesh was in the incongruous surroundings of a small tea-room not far from the British Museum. We had arranged to meet beneath the portico but in the event of either of us being delayed had suggested the alternative; in the event the Professor had missed his train and came on to the restaurant where I had already ordered tea.

It was one of those dim places, all pewter, brass and oak settles and as the Professor slumped into place opposite me, his back to the light, it took me some minutes to form an exact impression of his features. He was an enormous man, more than six feet three inches tall, I should have said, and proportionately broad. His hair was quite white but despite this I should not have put his age at more than about forty-five and he showed great vigour and determination in his movements and general aspect.

He had a small clipped Van Dyke beard, very clear blue eyes that seemed to look right through a man and his neat blue bow tie above his well-tailored grey suit re-echoed the eyes. Despite his height and bulk his figure was trim and athletic and I sensed that here was a man not only a scholar and deeply read in strange, out of the way subjects, but one well able to take care of himself in a tight corner. I felt somehow in my heart, even before he sat down, depositing a brown shooting-hat with game-birds feathers in the brim on the settle beside him, that I had already committed myself to his affairs, before he even broached the subject of our meeting.

We were on our third cup of tea and the last of the toasted scones before we engaged in general conversation. He had been sizing me up between the comings and goings of the waitress and I sensed also that I had met with his approval. He was an American, of course, but one of that type who seemed to belong to no special country or time; he lived nomadically, wherever he happened to have affairs that interested him. He was immensely wealthy and thus able to indulge his tastes and as he was unmarried and likely to remain so through choice, it did not matter where he made his abode.

As he spoke now his accent seemed to re-echo faintly the European rather than the American and then I remembered that despite his name – it had been Anglicised in his father's time – he came of old Central European stock. He touched at first on the general technicalities of the work I had been doing and I was astonished how much he knew about me and my career. He had even seen TO THE ENDS OF THE EARTH, the motion picture I had shot on the Luttrell Earth-Bores, and I gathered he had a print run for him at the Metropolitan Museum of Modern Art in New York. It is pleasant to be praised, particularly by so eminent a man in his field as Clark Ashton Scarsdale. Not that he was effusive; but his few clipped words of approbation amounted to the same thing in a person of his reticent character.

I said little; it was not my place to enlarge on my talents, small as they were, but I must confess his words warmed me; I wanted to draw him out as I felt sure there must be more to come.

He waited until we had finished the last of the pastries – I am particularly fond of those which have liberal quantities of Cornish clotted cream in their makeup – and then gave me a tight smile, which showed strong, even yellow teeth beneath the light beard.

"You must have thought this an incongruous place for a meeting," he ventured at length.

"On the contrary, this is just what I should have done in your place," I said.

"Oh." He folded his arms on the edge of the table and looked at me keenly.

"Neutral ground," I said. "If I hadn't fitted your requirements, you would merely have concluded the interview in a non-committal way and I should never have heard from you again."

I fancied I saw a faint flush start out on his cheeks but he merely observed coolly, "You have an admirable grasp of the situation, Mr Plowright. You are the man for me. I had already come to that conclusion and I propose to offer you the adventure of a lifetime."

My face must have looked as startled as the thoughts that were already chasing themselves through my mind, for he burst out laughing, causing a serious dent in the façade of the two old ladies at the next table. From the look on their faces they suspected an anarchist plot at the least.

"We cannot talk here," said the Professor, laying his hand on my arm. "I have some business at the Museum and then I will be in a position to put a proposition before you. One I think which will present some points of interest to a man of your character. I would suggest another meeting this day week at my home in Surrey, if the time and place suit you. You could then meet some of my colleagues and be able to make up your mind."

He scribbled some details on a card he took from an inside pocket; he slid it over and I glanced at the address. I had already made up my mind to go but put on a show of hesitation, though I don't really think it deceived him for a moment.

"An expedition," he said hesitantly, a half-smile at the corner of his mouth. "You will come?"

"I'll be there," I said at length.

He drew his breath in with a long gasp as though my going was important to him.

His hand crushed mine in a gesture of farewell and then he was gone, his enormous form stooping to dodge the irregularities in the beamed ceiling of the tea-shop.

I went home to sort out some of my photographic equipment and then sat up late smoking and pondering the nature of the Professor's next venture. It was nearly two a.m. before I gave it up and sought my bed. I would not have slept very soundly had I known exactly what the next few months were to bring.

Two

I

It was a wet, miserable afternoon, with a misty rain drifting across the countryside when I drove down to Surrey the following week.

I had taken lunch at Guildford and it still wanted a few minutes of two when I arrived at the Professor's residence. The Pines had not been imaginatively named but as I drove up a gravel drive between those trees, the white façade of a large Georgian house began to form itself in the drizzle beyond my windscreen. I had no intention of staying the night and I hoped, due to the weather conditions, that our conference would not take long. With the week's interim, the impact made by the Professor's personality had faded and I had partly forgotten the excitement generated by our conversation.

However, it rapidly revived when Scarsdale himself came out on to the great tiled porch to greet me; he dismissed the manservant who had come to open the door of my car, gave my hand a bone-shaking clasp and quelled the savage-looking dog that barked round my heels, all, it seemed, in one smooth movement.

"I hope you've come with an open mind," he said. "People I invite to become my collaborators always begin by raising so many sceptical objections. It does waste so much time, which is why I've been able to mount only two major enquiries in the past ten years."

"You'll find me a fairly amiable subject," I said placatingly. "I find it best merely to take the films or photographs and leave the theorising to those best qualified."

Scarsdale slammed the door of my car with a crash that set the dog barking again and his great eyes seemed to glow with enthusiasm.

"Admirable," he said. "Admirable. I'm hardly ever wrong in my analysis of character. We'll get along fine."

He led the way over towards the front door, the dog slinking at his heels. I followed him into a large tiled hallway, whose pastel-coloured walls were lined with sombre oil-paintings.

"Miserable brute," said Scarsdale as the man shut the door behind us. "He goes with the house."

His face creased with amusement as he looked at the expression on my face.

"The dog, man, the dog," he exclaimed and added, sotto voce, "Not Collins."

He flung open the door of a vast room containing thousands

of multi-coloured books that marched down three sides. A generous fire blazed cheerfully on the hearth but most of the heat came from radiators set against alcoves in the walls.

"You've eaten, I expect," said Scarsdale. "Well, I guess you'll not say no to coffee and a brandy after your drive."

I assented gratefully and sat on the arm of a leather chair before the fire while I absorbed the details of the room. One or two things about it struck me as decidedly curious for a library. There was a large buffet with silver chafing dishes set on it, against the long wall unoccupied by books. A bay window at one end commanded a fine view of misty countryside; a dining table was set in it. There were four places laid and the remains of a meal.

A sand-table occupied the immediate foreground of the study and there was also a green baize board attached to the wall near the buffet, which had notices pinned to it. The whole place reminded me of nothing more than an informal sort of military mess, used by a small group of officers. Scarsdale had evidently noted my puzzlement for he came back down the room bearing two giant-sized cups of steaming coffee. He put them down on a small mahogany table before the fire and went back for balloon glasses and the decanter.

We drank the coffee and brandy and indulged in small talk for a few minutes, the chill of my drive slowly receding. Scarsdale saw me look at the dining table and said quietly, "I have three colleagues in my current project, all personally selected. You'll be meeting them later. That is, if you agree to my proposition."

He finished his coffee and stood up. The dog, a wolfhound I took it to be, regarded him balefully from one yellow eye and showed its equally yellow teeth in a low growl. Then it sank its head back on the carpet before the fire and composed itself to sleep as Scarsdale and I took our glasses over towards the sand-table.

"What do you make of this?" the Professor said. I went round the other side to find the best light and examined the lay-out. My photographer's mind was already absorbing the information before me and noting the best position for pictures. What I saw was a series of mountain ranges on a colossal scale; these were set at one end of the table. A route was pegged through with pink tape and various labels in neatly-inked white card gave place-names. I noted two, Nylstrom and Zak, but I had no idea what country was supposed to be represented and the Professor volunteered no information, merely stood sipping his brandy and watching me from the other side of the table.

I walked farther down and followed the pink-taped route, which meandered up valleys and across gorges; the trail ended with a honeycomb segment of caves, which I examined with great care before passing on. There seemed to be about forty openings, grouped about one great central cave at ground level; if these were all to scale with the mountain range, the height of the main cave roof would have been about as big as St. Paul's Cathedral. I went round the table looking for any legend that would have indicated the country or the nature of the expedition but there was nothing.

I went back to my original position, watched silently by Scarsdale. A piece of timber had been placed across the sand-table at this point and the other half was given up to a clay surface. But the pink tape trail went on and I guessed, correctly, that the remainder of the model demonstrated in cutaway sections, the interior of the caverns. There was a stool standing near the buffet some way away and I went and got this and sat on it in order to study the project in greater detail. Scarsdale produced another stool and went and sat next to me but still said nothing.

The pink tape went along endless passages and alleyways before it came to an abrupt conclusion in the middle of a featureless circle of clay. In the middle of the oval space someone had scrawled a huge question mark with the point of a stick.

I had come to the end of my examination of this enigmatic construction and was about to put the first of my queries to my companion when we were suddenly interrupted by a curious noise. It was like a high, whining shriek and I followed Scarsdale as he rose and led me over to the window. The rain had cleared a little now and from farther down the slope of lawn, which dropped away to a lake in the distance, there was a fold of tumbled, orchard-like ground which had been left rough and full of weeds.

From out the tangled mass of grass and nettles the snout of an extraordinary grey machine was protruding. It poked its way like some blind animal finding its route; then the grasses parted and I could see tracks, something like a tank's, moving delicately as a caterpillar's legs beneath a metal skirt. A shutter slid back in the upper half of the structure, revealing an oval window. A head appeared in the conning tower or whatever it was, surveyed the landscape and the shutter slid to. The screaming of the engine increased, the thing turned and then a fence-post snapped off as the machine slid back down the slope from our view. Scarsdale swore. He went over to the fireplace and pressed a bell set in the moulding of the surround.

The manservant appeared with astonishing alacrity.

"Collins," said Scarsdale. "You might tell Dr Van Damm that I would appreciate him keeping to the agreed terrain and not invading the garden. I do not own the property, as he knows, and must pay for any damage."

"Certainly, Professor," said the attendant, as though the Professor's instruction were a long-standing one. He went out, closing the double-doors behind him.

"Now that you've seen our little exhibition," said the Professor, resuming his original seat by the fireside, "I'd like to tell you what my proposition is all about."

2

"I am not at liberty to divulge how I came by all my information," said Scarsdale, "but you may remember the occasion which first prompted my getting in touch with you."

"My photographs of the Crosby Patterson relics, if I remember rightly," I replied. "With particular reference to the inscriptions on the rock excavated from under the ice by Patterson's team."

"Precisely," said the Professor. "You may recall from the public prints of the time that I expressed great interest in the hieroglyphs. Not only was it extremely unlikely that such things could have been found in the Polar regions. I had another reason for my interest. You see, I had seen them before."

There was silence in the room for a while, broken only by the faint sputtering of logs on the hearth. The wolfhound appeared to be dreaming; his flanks were heaving and from time to time one of his hind legs gave a satisfied twitch.

The Professor drained the last of his brandy and looked round for the coffee percolator. He carefully poured himself half a cup and added sugar and cream before he went on.

"Some strange things have been happening in the world this past few years," he said. "Not only in the world but out there in space."

He indicated the window, with an expansive wave of his hand.

"Yet most of mankind seems absolutely oblivious of the implications. Do you remember what the Press were pleased to call the 'Scarsdale Lights'. Back in 1932."

"I seem to recall something of it now that you mention it," I said. "Weren't they put down to solar flares . . ."

Scarsdale interrupted me with an exasperated snort.

"I don't mean to be rude my dear fellow," he said. "But you really must learn to keep an open mind. I will just tell you the facts as I see them. Without the theorising behind them, you understand. That will come later. There will be much time, when we are out there. The solar flares, as you call them, were something much more. I have made a long study of the phenomena and it is my considered opinion – borne out by field research I might add – that the hieroglyph inscriptions appeared at the same time, in various parts of the world."

"From space you mean?" I asked him.

Scarsdale gave me a long, fierce look.

"Who knows?" he said. "If we could but read the inscriptions in their entirety we might possess the secrets of the universe. I believe, most sincerely, that the tablets are instructions of some sort, for beings who may visit our planet at some future time. Or who may even be amongst us as we sit here.

"This is why I was so interested in your pictures of the Patterson relics. I was already working on my own line of research; one that was cut short after I had made a promising beginning. The route you see on the sand-table there was traced by myself, with much labour and danger, just over a year ago. I cannot divulge its exact location, for reasons which will become apparent later, but

I believe it to be of vital importance to the future of our race. Or even to the survival of our race as we know it."

Scarsdale looked unusually serious as he made this pronouncement and he made an imperious figure as he sat before the fire in the gloom of the big study, the light from the shaded lamps catching the fleeting expressions of his face, half shadowed by the beard.

"This was why I chose you," he resumed after a moment. "You are not only a first-rate photographer and a man with a scholarly background who would understand my views. You also have other attributes which are admirable for my purposes. You have physical courage, youth and strength, and you have already demonstrated your spirit of adventure by seeking out the tasks you have already accomplished. All of which taken together adds up to a pretty convincing package from my point of view.

"The three scientists I have already chosen to accompany me are first-rate people and eminent in their own fields, but none of them have the physical strength necessary for certain aspects of our task. That will have to be up to you and I. I need at least one other man who is a man of action, an adventurer as well as a technician. My own capabilities I have already proved to my satisfaction. Are you game?"

"I don't know what the devil you're driving at, Professor," I said. "Neither do I know where we're going or what we're going to do when we get there, but I wouldn't miss this trip for anything. As long as I'm able to photograph and you indicate the sort of equipment I'm likely to need, that's all that matters to me."

The Professor struck his thigh with a long sigh and clasped me by the hand. The gesture was a theatrical one and he drew his hand away almost immediately with a muttered apology as though he were ashamed of the movement, yet it was a perfectly apposite one. He did look like a man who was worried over his future plans and it did also appear that my agreement had solved his particular problems.

I smiled and said that though I had now agreed to come and that nothing would turn me from my purpose so long as he wanted me, I would still like to know more about the project. I appreciated that he didn't yet want to tell us where we were going and the precise nature of our enquiries but I would be interested to hear more of the enigmatic matters of which he had already hinted.

Scarsdale sat back in his chair and drained his coffee cup before replying.

"The lights," he said. "I have been engaged in research for many years on such matters. My particular line of inquiry directed me to the remote region for which we are bound. After a great deal of difficulties – some of them, I am compelled to say, caused by my own ignorance and foolhardiness at the time of which I am speaking, I achieved a partial success. The expedition I am mounting, plus the skills of its members combined with the special equipment, much of which I have myself designed, should now be able to score a complete success."

Scarsdale paused again and then went on. "You will find some strangeness, I daresay. The title of the project is the Great Northern Expedition. Yet we are not going north. This is a purely diversionary measure designed to placate the press and the wider world. The scientists and other colleagues who have long sneered at my efforts in this field, may think and say what they will. But secrecy as to our intentions is a prime necessity. I must ask you to behave with the utmost discretion and must also urge you to move in here with us within the next week. This is in order that you may train with your companions and get to know us well before we embark."

He looked at me enigmatically for a moment.

"You have no ties, I take it? A fiancée, sweetheart or . . . ?"

"Any other entanglement," I finished for him. "No, there is nothing of that sort. I am a completely free agent. I have a permanent housekeeper in London and my solicitor looks after my affairs. I am often away for long periods, so there will be nothing new in your business."

Scarsdale nodded satisfaction.

"As a matter of interest how long should we expect to be away?" I asked him.

"At least a year," was his reply, given without the slightest hesitation. "It goes without saying that proper contracts will be drawn for your signature before we leave England. And the commercial value of your photographs and films will be your own, once we have made arrangements for our own material."

"That is extremely generous of you, Professor," I said. "We may take everything as agreed then, apart from detail."

We had just risen to our feet when there was a crash at the door and a tall, thin form stood in the entrance. The worried face of Collins could be seen at the intruder's elbow.

"By God, Scarsdale, this is a definite liberty!" said a high, thin voice like a woman's. "How are we to master these extraordinary contraptions if we can't manoeuvre without you worrying about some damn potato patch."

"Come in, Van Damm," said Scarsdale smoothly, propelling me forward down the room.

"I'd like you to meet the newest member of the expedition."

Three

I

Cornelius Van Damm was, as I have indicated, tall and thin, but it was not only his fluting, effeminate voice that had such an extraordinary effect upon those meeting him for the first time. When we had both exchanged nods, perfunctorily acknowledging Scarsdale's sketchy introduction, and the Professor had brought us all back towards the fireside, I had more leisure to study him. Both he and Scarsdale engaged in a form of bickering which I later came to realise was a pose, a role both played to the full; the Professor emphasised his virile, bear-like qualities while the doctor developed a waspish querulousness which suited his squeaky voice.

Underneath it all lay a profound theatricality, a streak common to both men; both were distinguished in their own spheres; in addition to being a first-class electrical engineer, Van Damm was learned in many fields, being also a geologist and metallurgist as well as a fine revolver and rifle shot. He was to find his talents fully exercised on the Great Northern Expedition.

Fortunately, neither of the two remaining members, whom I had yet to meet, had such temperaments as those of Van Damm and the Professor; they preferred to leave the limelight to the two prima donnas, and were both immensely practical and phlegmatic by nature, which was no doubt why Scarsdale had selected them in the first instance. As for myself, I had no great axe to grind, as I have already indicated, and preferred merely to observe and practice my own specialised subject of photography.

Now, as the two men snapped at one another in the firelight, the older man biting off his words like a pike swallowing a tasty morsel, the Professor blandly riding rough-shod over the other's objections, I was amusedly summing up the doctor. What I saw was a man of exceedingly gaunt aspect; with a great craggy face, from which a pair of humorous brown eyes shone from within deep sockets. His thin sandy hair grew evenly over his scalp so that his skull resembled nothing so much as a pineapple; a delicate wisp of moustache bisected his face and a gold pince-nez, depending from a delicate silver chain, dangled from his third waistcoat button. He wore a green corduroy jacket, the waistcoat was of some dark brown material, and his trousers were of grey flannel. Over the whole was a sort of long brown dustcoat, such as that worn by stockmen or cattle-drovers in the Old West, and the dark brown riding boots, stained with mud, which completed his outfit, marked him as one of the oddest and most individual of men.

However, he presently grew calmer and seeming to recollect my presence, turned to me and grasped me by the hand; still with a red flush on his cheeks and a slight stammer in his voice, when he turned to interject an occasional remark at the Professor, he proved himself an entertaining speaker. Later I was to discover that his eccentric exterior concealed one of the kindliest of men.

However, all he said initially was, "You will find this a difficult sort of contract, Plowright. If we had a different leader, well then, that would simplify matters and one could guarantee success. But with such a boorish and obtuse person as Scarsdale, I will be extremely surprised if we achieve what we set out to do."

I had expected the Professor to reply with some monstrous outburst but to my intense surprise he merely threw back his bearded head and bellowed with laughter like a bull.

"You never disappoint me, Van Damm," he chuckled at length. He glanced over at me. "Mark my words, my dear fellow, we shall have an admirable expedition."

Then he rang for Collins to clear the table and we all went back into the hall.

"While the doctor is demolishing a few more pear trees I daresay you'd like to come and meet the remainder of your colleagues," Scarsdale said smoothly. "You'll find them much more amiable."

His latter remark was within Van Damm's hearing; the tall man stood with his feet planted apart at one side of the hall and I was even more surprised when I saw him smile appreciatively at the Professor's disparaging comment. I began to understand the two men a little better as I followed the Professor out onto the front drive; he led the way around the house, our feet crunching in the gravel, until we came to a cobbled courtyard and a sort of stable, together with a group of outbuildings. From the latter came the low hum of machinery.

In the centre of the courtyard was standing one of the strange grey machines I had already seen, being demonstrated by Van Damm in the orchard below the house. The Professor looked at me keenly but there was no faltering in his even stride.

"There'll be time for that later," he said. "We have a lot to do this afternoon and you'll not be wanting to get back to town too late."

I protested that I had all the time in the world, my previous reservations quite forgotten, so exciting and unusual did I find this new world, with its sense of mysterious purpose and urgency. Most of this, like an electric current, was flowing from the figure of the Professor himself, of course, and I was later to find that he affected almost everyone in the same way; even Van Damm was not immune, though he had learned to disguise his true feelings with an air of bickering criticism.

At a long bench in the interior of the workshop two men were sitting. The older looked round as we entered and a broad smile spread across his face. He jumped up impulsively and said to Scarsdale, "You were right, Professor. The wavelength made all the difference. I've ironed out the difficulties."

The Professor smiled and turned to me, making the formal introductions.

"This is Norman Holden. Apart from being an excellent historian, he's our radio expert. Van Damm will be responsible for maintaining the tractors."

Holden was a man of about fifty-five, of medium height and stockily built; he had even white teeth, a rather fleshy mouth and broad-set eyes of a deep brown. He had character and good humour in his face and I liked him immediately.

The other man at the end of the bench got up and came towards us. Geoffrey Prescott was about forty-five; an expert linguist and specialist in Egyptology, he also had his strictly practical side. He would attend to map-making and cooking on the expedition and could apply his talents in a number of other directions. Fortunately, Scarsdale himself was also a doctor of medicine and could deal with any serious ills which might befall our little band.

Prescott, I later understood from Scarsdale had helped decipher something of the hieroglyphs which had so intrigued the Professor and which had been the means of our meeting. Just now he excused himself from joining in our conversation; his current work demanded all his attention if the expedition was to get away on time. He looked at Scarsdale with an enthusiastic smile as he spoke and with a wave of his hand went back to the end of the bench. Scarsdale said nothing but got out a blackened old pipe from his pocket and bit at its yellow stem.

We had been walking round the workshop and found ourselves near the door to the yard; there was another vast shed, like an aeroplane hangar adjoining and Scarsdale now put his bull-like shoulder to a sliding door and slid it shudderingly back. He moved about ahead of me, switching on lights.

"Excellent people, Prescott and Holden," he said succinctly. "One couldn't wish for better companions. You'll fit in well, I think."

I stood blinking in the sudden glare of light from the banks of powerful reflectors set in the ceiling girders. Before me were two of the great grey tractor vehicles; these, unlike the one I had seen in the yard and the other in the orchard earlier, were shining with new paint and carried registration numbers. Both bore the stencilled black lettering, GREAT NORTHERN EXPEDITION. Number 1, I saw was labelled Command Vehicle and had Scarsdale's name beneath. Number 2, bore Dr Van Damm's name as commander. Numbers three and four would be accompanying us as reserve vehicles, explained Scarsdale, ushering me up the light metal steps into his own craft.

Once inside the sliding doors, the Professor switched on the interior lighting and showed me his domain with somewhat justifiable pride.

"We have developed these vehicles between the four of us, to overcome certain difficulties I have already encountered," said the Professor. "A new principle of friction-drive is incorporated in the tractor units. Van Damm, whatever his faults in other directions, was invaluable here. He also developed a new type of long-life heavy duty battery, which we are able to re-charge en route."

As he spoke, he showed me round the interior of the craft which seemed to me extremely ingenious and spacious. The control room, which had observation windows masked by sliding metal shutters, also incorporated a sort of chart-table and a rack for all the Professor's books and instruments.

Beyond was a bedroom which could sleep three crew-members in comfort; beyond that again a small galley fully equipped for cooking. There was even a minute toilet and shower stall and wash-basin.

"The other tractors are identical," said the Professor, "so that if something happens to one we can merely change over without difficulties of any sort."

He paused before he went on.

"You have no objection to learning to handle the machine, I suppose?"

"I should be delighted," I said. "I intend to make myself fully useful in addition to my photographic duties."

"I ask for a particular reason," Scarsdale said. "The machines will go with us by sea in the first instance, of course. To get them to our destination means that we must have a driver for each. That commits four out of five, with one man acting as cook and reserve driver. So you can see we shall need the help of everyone."

"You won't be engaging the help of any porters?" I said.

The Professor shook his head.

"You will see the reason why in due course," he replied. "We must have another two months in England before embarking. As you have seen, Van Damm is still far from perfect at piloting these things and I'm sure you'll want to be thoroughly conversant before taking over."

I agreed. Then another thought struck me.

"As I'm to be the official photographer, ought I not to record some of these preparations on film?" I said. "I have my equipment outside and would be delighted to start this afternoon."

The Professor looked pleased but then his face clouded over. He put his hand on my shoulder.

"I'm sure you won't take this amiss, my dear fellow, but I must rely on your discretion."

"I'm not quite sure I follow you," I replied.

The Professor operated the mechanism which let down the shutters from in front of the forward windows. There was the hum of electric motors in this warm little world which seemed remote from the wet Surrey countryside about us.

"This is a highly secret project," Scarsdale continued. "I'm at great pains that it should remain so. If the Press should get wind of it, there might be difficulties involved in the country for which we are heading. So your prints must be shown to no-one but myself and your colleagues here."

So worried did he look that I readily gave him my assurance, adding that if he wished I would leave the undeveloped film with him and print the material with my own equipment the next time I came down.

He seemed pleased at this but as I left the tractor to seek my camera, he halted me at the doorway.

"To be quite fair to you, Plowright, I will tell you a little more about this business before you go. My conscience will then be clear."

I assured him that I had already made up my mind to accompany him as official photographer but if he liked to let me know more about his plans and the circumstances surrounding the expedition, then I would, of course, fully respect any confidences he cared to place in me.

2

The next hour was an extremely busy one; I took something like seventy photographs in that time, with particular regard to the detail of the specialised equipment Scarsdale and Van Damm had perfected. I knew this would be appreciated by the Professor. He, together with the scowling Van Damm was persuaded to pose together on the steps of one of the tractors. Then I went out again into the drizzling rain to photograph Van Damm's extraordinary manoeuvres in the orchard, watched by an alarmed Collins, who had strict orders from Scarsdale to report even so much as a bruised pear from the fruit trees.

I went on from there back to the workshop where I recorded the others at work, until I had a fairly comprehensive picture record of the Great Northern Expedition's activities to date. By this time it was five o'clock and I was already so far committed to the as yet mysterious preparations of my companions that I was delighted when the Professor suggested that I should stay the night and at once fell in with his suggestion.

One of Collins' stranger duties was the formal serving of tea, complete with silver teapot and all the accoutrements of toast, crumpets and scones, among the rough surroundings of the workshop, when the scientists were too busy to come indoors to the house. He had a strange contraption like a hospital trolley, with a collapsible hood to keep the rain from his heated delicacies and he trundled this solemnly out to the courtyard at five o'clock.

So it was that I found myself sipping almost boiling tea from fine china at the chart-table of the Professor's tractor while he sombrely explained to me something of the difficulties we would be facing. He repeated that he had been somewhat alerted to the dangers facing the world by his researches into certain forbidden books many years before, in the early twenties. It was not until very much later that he began to connect them with the inscriptions found on stone tablets in various parts of the world; and then, eventually, with last year's strange spring; the shifting lights in the sky, which were observed almost on a global scale and which were connected, Scarsdale maintained, with something he called the Coming.

It was such a spring and such a sequence of events, he said, which were hinted at in blasphemous old books and forbidden treatises in Arabic and Hebrew which he had studied for years on end and which he eventually made to yield up their secrets. It was the Latin volume, The Ethics of Ygor, he added, which had produced the most worthwhile results of his research; and the key-signs and notably the Magnetic Ring which was said to spin beyond the farthest suns of the universe, had eventually been the cause of his stumbling on to some fantastic and unbelieveable facts which the Professor hesitated even to mention to his most learned colleagues.

They concerned, Scarsdale believed, a portion of the universe which he called "the great white space"; it was an area which the Old Ones particularly regarded with awe and which they had always formally referred to, in their primeval writings as The Great White Space. This was a sacred belt of the cosmos through which beings could come and go, as through an astral door, and which was the means of conquering dizzying billions of miles of distance which would have taken even the Old Ones thousands of years to traverse.

Scarsdale believed he had discovered a key to the identity of the Old Ones, through the hieroglyphs discovered on earth and after long and profound study of the writings, coupled with the key books of The Ethics of Ygor, he had come to the conclusion that the riddle of their existence might be probed here on earth. It was then that he had set out on the first and most difficult of his exploratory journeys, which he had already mentioned.

If Scarsdale feared that I should disbelieve what to a layman might appear to be a somewhat wild narrative, my demeanour must have rapidly given him confidence, for he was able to speak more clearly and confidently as the minutes ticked past. For my part I had no cause to doubt his sincerity or sanity and the distinction of his colleagues on the expedition, plus the sober and impressive scientific preparations going ahead, were evidence in themselves that something serious and solidly based was afoot.

He searched for reassurance in my eyes and my continued silence encouraging him, he continued. We must have made a strange sight, he large and bearded, myself with one fragile china cup in my hand; the pair of us in earnest conclave within the conning tower of a grey metal tractor in a large shed set in the midst of the drizzling Surrey uplands. Yet neither of us thought it incongruous so sincerely did Scarsdale believe the truth of what he was relating; and no less sincerely did I receive his confidences.

"Believe me, Plowright, if I could at this stage reveal the exact location of our destination I would do so," he said, fixing me earnestly with those arresting eyes. "Too much is at stake. Let me just say, for the sake of coherence that it was Peru. It was not Peru, but no matter. I had spent years working on my calculations. There was no doubt in my mind that they were correct. My problem was that the need for secrecy meant my party must be small; there were but three of us. To my great sorrow and misfortune, there was treachery on the part of a local agent I trusted; my two companions fell sick. Foolishly, I decided to go on with the large party of porters. I had to engage bearers as the vast amount of equipment made it a necessity. Had I had the present vehicles, well then, I should have succeeded triumphantly. As it was, my efforts were foredoomed to failure."

Scarsdale was not a man given to emotion, as I later came to know, but the recollection evidently moved him for his voice trembled and he drummed impatiently with strong, spatulate fingers on the chart table before him. He recollected himself and the impassive exterior resumed itself again.

"The wonder of it is that I got so far," he said. "I gained the mountains and the outer caves before the porters deserted. I won't go into details because I want every man of you to start this venture with a fresh, clear mind. But there were the inscriptions, there the tunnels you have seen in the library of the house; I took a pack and some provisions and marking my way, I went on. The nights were the worst. I spent many days in the tunnels and I slept badly. Then I came to a vast underground lake; and there, hunger, plus the sheer physical impossibility of continuing without specialist equipment, overcame me. I almost failed to make it, I was so weak by the time I gained the outer air. Fortunately, some of the guides had remained on the mountain and brought me down. The full affair never got into the papers. And that's about it."

He pointed out through the thick quartz windows to the far side of the hangar.

"Collapsible rubber boats of specially toughened material. If necessary, four of them, suitably girdered could act as pontoons for ferrying tractors. I don't think we'll fail this time. We dare not fail."

He clenched his fist on the table in front of him as he spoke and it seemed to me as though shutters momentarily closed over his eyes, but not before I had seen chaotic fires burning within. I then realised that Clark Ashton Scarsdale was a man of immense strength whose mental fortitude was under siege by equally strong pressures. I cleared my throat and the trivial sound seemed to recall the Professor to his surroundings. It appeared to me then as though he had been far away physically, and that once again he stood upon the shore of a vast tideless underground sea.

"The clay oval upon the model depicts the underground lake?" I said.

The Professor nodded. "Exactly. I could, in fact, have gone beyond this in the model but I did not feel it politic to do so."

Seeing the surprise upon my face he went on.

"I have formulated theories from my earlier research but as I have myself not seen with my own eyes what lies beyond the lake it seemed pointless to give it physical features in a model of that sort."

"What do you expect to find beyond the lake?" I asked bluntly.

Scarsdale smiled. He became at once far less serious.

"I have, as I indicated, definite theories. What these are it would be both premature and unwise to reveal at this stage. It might take the zest out of the exploration for the other members of the expedition. And we must, must we not, have some speculative topics to discuss during the long nights in camp?"

I agreed. Just one point of curiosity remained for the moment.

"The tractors, Professor. Supposing we venture beyond visual touch?"

Scarsdale became the practical man again.

"Powerful searchlights for underground work, plus lanterns for pre-arranged signals. Short-wave radio sets for verbal contact, effective up to a range of five miles. You'll be given instructions on this equipment also before we start. But here's Collins. He'll be wanting the tea-things. Are you satisfied with the Great Northern Expedition?"

"Perfectly," I said.

Thus casually did I commit myself to the most appalling experience of my life.

Four

I

Having completed my arrangements in London I drove back down to Surrey the following week in a mood which blended contentment with apprehension. In the interim I had time to consider the implications of the Professor's cryptic statements; divorced of his personality and the sincerity of his voice they left a good deal to be desired. And yet, wild as some of his assertions had been and as mysterious as our destination still appeared, I was inclined on balance to believe him. There was no doubt of his sanity in my mind and his field record was an impressive one.

I had been to the reference books during the past few days and my old friend Robson had added his own personal reminiscences of Scarsdale's personality; third-hand, I must admit, but they had reinforced my own belief in his integrity. Robson too was a dabbler in outré and bizarre things on the fringe of the world's knowledge; one of his own friends had accompanied Scarsdale on what he was pleased to call one of his "hikes". He was full of admiration for a man he regarded as one of the most outstanding field workers of the twentieth century.

All this was good enough for me. With Robson's assurance that he would "look in" at my flat from time to time and deal with any mail of a business nature, and my own promise that I would write as and when I was able, I packed my few personal belongings, together with a plethora of photographic equipment, bundled it all in my old car and set off. On my arrival at The Pines I was at once flung into such a routine of work, research, preparation and tests that on looking back I regard it as one of the most enjoyable – if occasionally traumatic experiences – of my life.

In addition to my special photographic work – and I had to set up a minute dark room for my own purposes in Number 1 tractor – and the general manhandling of supplies inescapable in such a project where the five principals are desirous of keeping their preparations secret – I had also to learn the mysteries of tractor driving, plus the operation of the radio equipment linking the mobile bases. Scarsdale, to my surprise, had designated me his sole companion in Number 1 with Van Damm in charge of Number 2, Holden and Prescott acting as his crew. I asked if that were not causing an imbalance among the expedition's scientific personnel but the Professor's reply somewhat startled me.

"The technical qualifications have little to do with this aspect," he assured me. "All I am concerned with is that the two physically strongest people shall be in the leading vehicle."

This factor, together with the other special equipment being loaded, filled me with some disquiet. Rifles, revolvers, grenades, Very pistols and even what looked like a rack of elephant guns were among the formidable armaments being screwed into position within the vehicles.

I had meant to ask Scarsdale about this but something in his eyes made me hold my own counsel. Certainly, none of the others saw any reason for comment or alarm in the material currently loading and I wondered if perhaps they had discussed it all earlier. I understood the four of them had been at the Surrey house for something like a year and certainly they all worked smoothly together, with a score of private jokes and special references that

I, as a newcomer, could not be expected to comprehend.

The only outward opinion expressed was Holden's jocular remark to Prescott one afternoon. Scarsdale was absent on some business in Guildford and Holden was lifting one of the massive elephant pieces through the sliding door of Number 2. He made some grave comment about Van Damm's forthcoming "sparrow shoot". To my surprise both he and his companion went into veritable paroxysms of laughter and the subject of their amusement, whom I had not earlier seen in the hangar doorway, joined in, Van Damm's high, snickering laugh echoing among the roof girders.

They had more cause for amusement shortly as it was soon discovered that I was an even more inept pupil than Van Damm at tractor-driving; try as I would, I could not at first remember exactly how to operate the two confounded levers and the complicated gear-stick that Scarsdale and Van Damm had devised to drive the things and my efforts in the misty orchard, with Collins hopping frantically out of the way and the Professor bellowing about the high cost of fruit trees, raised echoes of mirth long after their physical manifestations had ceased.

Van Damm, I think, was secretly pleased at this, as it gave the Professor another scapegoat though he did not, of course, bully me in the same manner and his arguments did not take the same form that his mock rows with the doctor took. But he did take me aside on one or two occasions to express his gentle concern at my ineptitude and it was this, more than anything, which forged in me the ambition to succeed. That I succeeded in becoming the best driver among them, with a ground-work of only three weeks' training, was a tribute, I feel, to the Professor's personality rather than to any special aptitude on my part.

When the Professor went to the bank one morning to draw out a number of charts, books and other documents he had deposited there, we then knew that the time of departure must be near. We were not leaving, initially, by ship, but the Professor had arranged for the vehicles to be taken through France and Italy by road, in three great lorries and we could, of course, leave at almost any time, being subject to no sailing schedules other than those maintained by the Channel boats.

We ourselves were flying to Rome where the Professor intended to carry out certain field trials in a desolate sandy region to the north of the city. I think Collins was the most disappointed person at The Pines on learning that he was not to accompany the Professor. Scarsdale told him one afternoon when the lugubrious manservant was helping to break down the sand-table model a few days before our departure. We would miss Collins also, as his stiff, correct figure, always trying to maintain protocol in face of chaos was a never-ending source of good-natured amusement among us.

But Collins brightened when Scarsdale told him he needed someone he could trust to maintain the house while he was abroad and with the promise of a bonus in addition to complete sovereignty over the large domestic staff of ten which ran the place, he went about his duties with renewed vigour.

All went as Scarsdale had planned. I had no-one or nothing in particular to keep me in England and so it was no great hardship for me to forsake my native shore for a protracted period; all the other members of the expedition were bachelors – no doubt specially chosen by the Professor for that reason – and the only person among us who had the least tie was Holden, who had become engaged to be married a short while before I arrived at The Pines.

Scarsdale and Van Damm supervised the loading of the tractors; how the Professor avoided national press mention during this phase of the operation I never did discover. He had, I believe, given out originally that the Great Northern Expedition was to carry out tests in Europe before going to the Arctic and it may be that these latest manoeuvres were thought of little public interest, the newspapers reserving coverage for the expedition proper. I remained at The Pines with our three companions, where we concluded our packing and other minor tasks while awaiting the return of the two leaders from Dover.

The whole party flew out three days later to Italy by flying boat; we were accommodated at a private hotel near Ostia and, with the arrival of our precious vehicles a day or so after, carried out the sand trials as Scarsdale had decreed. We were there no more than a week and it would sorely overburden this narrative if I went into great detail over the tests, except to say that they were highly satisfactory.

Scarsdale and Van Damm also were extremely pleased with results, so much so that they occasionally forgot to bicker and our farewell dinner in Rome was such a convivial occasion that they even posed for a friendly photograph for one of the Continental society magazines. I thought I had acquitted myself fairly well; I had piloted my tractor up and down the dunes with a minimum of fuss and problems. In fact all four machines had handled extremely well and we had also tested the rubber boats in a fair breeze off Ostia one afternoon and results here had been pleasing. Scarsdale was particularly concerned over the short-wave radio links and the air conditioning units and the results again in both these departments had given us all cause for satisfaction.

The tractors were then driven to the docks at dead of night and loaded on to a freighter, destination unknown to us at the time. We also took passage on the same vessel and all public records of the Great Northern Expedition of 1933 then ceased. Where we went and exactly where we disembarked I am still not at liberty to disclose to the world and I will leave the reader to judge whether or not I have done that same world a disservice.

The fact remains that I did not – I dare not – be more specific and the reasons for this will emerge during the course of this narrative. The colours will inevitably grow more sombre with the drawing near of our party to that cursed country and those cursed mountains. The reader will appreciate by what I have already said that we went not to the north, but to the east. And at our going all the humour, the sunshine and the friendly comradeship that we had enjoyed amid the misty hills of Surrey seemed to evaporate as though they had never existed.

This is not to say that we did not remain kind to one another or that we no longer worked together as a coherent team, but that on our disembarkation from our long voyage, which lasted over a month, a sense of strain, a waiting expectancy and – eventually – a covert watching for *something*, had replaced the easy companionship of the earlier months. We disembarked in dismal conditions of tropical heat, we engaged porters, we started for the interior.

Further weary weeks passed; weeks in which heat, insects and petty pilfering among the porters were our principal worries. I am at liberty to say that we bordered Tibet but from there onwards nothing would induce me to reveal our destination. We pushed ahead for weeks more, the weather becoming cooler as we rose higher among the foothills. The lush, semi-tropical vegetation was giving way to more arid landscapes in which rock, ice-cold mountain streams and ancient beds of volcanic ash abounded. The colder weather was, of course, a relief after the sticky heat of the plains and we benefited greatly from this.

The four tractors behaved well and we were able to maintain an average speed of about 10 miles an hour on the mountain tracks, which was exceptionally good for this type of terrain. In fact so impressive was the performance that I once overheard Scarsdale praising Van Damm's design capabilities to his face. Looking back on it all I often wonder if something was not assisting nature to draw us inexorably forward to our sombre destination. Who knows? Certainly, a pulsing rhythm, which seemed to have a life of its own was the drum-beat which underlined the thin, high scream of the dynamos which propelled us forward daily, ever higher, ever onwards, ever towards the dark, menacing line of the distant mountains. There, Scarsdale said, we should pay off our porters and establish a provisional base at the ancient city of Zak.

Five

I

We reached Zak on September 1st and there, with much haggling and grumbling the porters were paid off. I will describe this old walled town with its Moorish-style architecture at some length a little later. For the moment we were tired with our long journey and the constant pull of the levers over the mountain trails induced a sort of sickness in those of us who had been driving. We were able, naturally, to rest at periods during the day, as we had to halt frequently to allow the porters to catch up with us, but nevertheless it was a blessed relief to learn that Scarsdale intended to stay here a week.

We would be able to enjoy fresh fruit and vegetables again as the people of this high plateau had conditions necessary for husbandry and were renowned in the area for the quality of their provisions. We would need to conserve our strength also, for the first of our tests was before us. In a small and necessarily brief council of war the Professor held in his command tractor on the evening of our arrival, he informed us that we would be setting out across the desert to Nylstrom, the last inhabited place before we jumped off into the unknown.

This was no less than 200 kilometres away and I looked at the Professor with something approaching awe; for had he not told me something of his previous explorations in this area? And, if I had heard him aright, he would at that time have been proceeding on foot. Even with the help of the porters who had remained on the mountain and who were no doubt familiar with the desert, it was a formidable achievement. I remembered Robson's friend and his talk of the Professor's "hikes"; formidable indeed. I looked at him again with even greater respect, if that were possible.

For the next few days we enjoyed such amenities the town was able to offer. We lived in the tractors, of course, but were able to supplement our somewhat monotonous tinned diet with the fruit and vegetables for which Zak was locally famous; Van Damm and the others worked on the maintenance of the tractors, in preparation for the desert crossing, while I recorded our new surroundings on film. The Professor held several conferences during the week we were resting and though he and the others went into great detail on the technical problems we might encounter, not once did anyone deal directly with what faced us or indeed what was the exact purpose of the Great Northern Expedition.

This was one of the main curiosities of the business, but on one of our last evenings Scarsdale did draw me aside to reiterate the importance – and the secrecy – of our project. Here, for the first time in Zak, our great water tanks, each capable of holding over a thousand gallons, were filled for the desert crossing. The water was first boiled and then chemically purified, according to an elaborate ritual laid down by Van Damm and the Professor. The people of Zak, who were a curious race with long, pointed heads something like the ancient Egyptians were the most stolid and indifferent people I had ever encountered; not only were they completely unco-operative so far as photographs of themselves were concerned, but completely uninterested in ourselves or in the doings of the Great Northern Expedition. This was all the more astonishing to me as they had never even seen a motor vehicle in their lives, let alone such remarkable vehicles as those we were driving.

With their dark, conical hats, and white, beribboned clothing very much like pyjama tops worn with plus-fours and soft leather bootees, they were a reserved and sullen lot, though the women included some notable beauties. The girls particularly were white-skinned and given to revealing one nipple only, in their specially designed clothing, which to a Westerner was extremely provocative. Not that Scarsdale had any need to issue the warning he felt necessary to mention the first evening we were there; the hard, proud attitude of the men and the murderous disembowelling knives they carried sheathed in brass-studded scabbards at their belts would have discouraged the most ardent admirer of their womenfolk.

They were, however, among themselves completely polygamous. Though some women preferred three or four husbands and to reserve their favours alone for them, we did note some of the more prominent citizens who had eight or more wives, all under the age of twenty. Fortunately for us, such co-operation as we needed from the populace, was secured by the local ruler, the Mir of Zak, whom Scarsdale had met on his previous visit. He was an extremely jovial man, for these people, that is; over seven feet tall and proportionately broad, he made us welcome and insisted that we park our vehicles within the walls of his palace.

This extraordinary building had six courtyards with very fine tesselated pavements; the Palace itself was surrounded by a wall of pink granite over twenty feet high and the sun beat back pitilessly from the pavement of the enclosure so that we at first regretted the hospitality which had forced us to accept this arid spot. However, when Scarsdale had pointed out our difficulties to the Mir, he had our tractors removed to a shady inner court, where fountains of clear water tinkled into lead basins and where strange vegetation, with scarlet and green fruits, grew in riotous profusion.

The Palace itself was built of some sort of white volcanic rock or ash, compressed into bricklets, so that it looked like nothing more than a giant wedding cake; at certain times of day it was dangerous to the eyes to look directly at it, so blinding was the light it reflected from the sun, and our party had to wear smoked goggles when we were within the Palace grounds.

The town of Zak bestrode the plateau in a commanding position; it was a very ancient and even handsome place with its white and honey coloured buildings and the clouds of pink birds, rather like doves, which inhabited its towers and courts, and which occasionally exploded into the air so that the thousands of birds circling the city looked like a second sunset as the desert sun stained their plumage red. There were no less than ten thousand inhabitants of Zak and the people there still carried on a fairly sophisticated civilisation; there were about a hundred land-owners and many of the people of the city went out daily to work on the farms which were extremely fertile, notwithstanding the savage sun, and richly irrigated by an elaborate water-works system controlled from the city.

The Mir, in laboured conversations conducted through Scarsdale told us something of his people's customs and history and promised that he would supply a guide to help us on our difficult journey across the desert to Nylstrom. There were even, if Scarsdale's translations were to be believed, civil servants, shopkeepers and many other grades of citizen, administrators and law-makers, within the walls of Zak. We looked, admired, strolled about the old town but avoided too close contact with the people. One could not explain it but one felt it necessary, despite the charm of the town itself. Our innate distrust of the people of Zak was something that was never to leave us.

2

Naturally, as we were thrown into close contact with one another, I was beginning to learn more about my companions. Dr Van

Damm and Scarsdale, now that they were in the field, were working more harmoniously together which proved to me that their
acidulous exchanges in England were little more than a pose. I had,
of course, had more opportunity to observe my colleagues during
the few weeks we had been working together in England and had
grown to like them all in their different ways.

We had been together on board ship of course, but many other
people were there as well; now, on the trip up to Zak we had each
of us been alone, concentrating on steering and controlling the
tractors, so that in the evenings, when we made camp, we were
glad to re-establish contact once again. Now, in Zak, for the first
time in our lives we were together and free of all but the most
nominal duties for several days. Inevitably, we got to know a great
deal more about each other in that brief space of time, than had
been possible hitherto.

I had a field day for photography and utilising my companions
as pack-mules was about the city early and late, photographing
and filming for the records; I also intended to produce a moving
picture of our activities and though Scarsdale and Van Damm
grumbled at having to go through simple motions over and over
again, until I had secured the material I wanted, I think they were
secretly pleased at this chronicle of what should turn out to be an
important step in man's fumbling advances towards knowledge.

Holden and Prescott tended to spend much of their time
together; as they had once held scientific appointments with the
same instrument manufacturing company, their friendship dated
from many years earlier and was entirely understandable.

Scarsdale and I were within a decade of the same age but he
was the leader of the party and his scientific and more abstruse
interests meant that he and Van Damm had far more in common,
despite the great discrepancy in their ages. Thus it was that I found
myself the odd man out; no-one, of course, emphasised this in any
way and it did not matter at all. I preferred it, in fact, and it meant
that I could go about my photographic errands without having to
wait on the whims or preferences of others.

I often spent my evenings on the windy edge of the plateau,
which was one of the most interesting places in Zak; there, on

a knife-edge of honey-coloured rock, I could look out across the desert, while on the other side, just below me in a fertile valley was the irrigation plant which fed the crops and the tall, curiously constructed windmills, with their irregular-shaped vanes which pumped the water along the dykes to the fields.

The high whine of the pumping machinery; the keening of the wind far out; the curious patterns and whorls in the browny-grey sand of the desert which stretched away across the far horizon; the black and menacing line of the mountains in the distance; and the scorching breath of an oven which came from off the desert like the respiration of a wild beast had a fascination all its own and even now, after all this time, and with the knowledge I bear, I have only to close my eyes to bring it all vividly back to mind. These evenings represented almost the last peaceful moments I was to know in this life.

So the days slowly passed in this strange spot with all the gentle inconsistency of a hashish-eater's dream and one evening Scarsdale announced that we would be setting out for the distant fastness of Nylstrom the following morning. We had spent the day testing the tractors and taking on fresh supplies so it was no real surprise but one had become so used to the present life that it was something of a shock to realise that we would shortly be fighting at the levers of the tractors and sweltering in the tropical heat.

The Mir had assigned to us one of the more prepossessing of his subjects, the dwarf Zalor, who knew the people of Nylstrom and, what was more important, the nomadic desert tribes, and who, the ruler thought, would be useful to us on our travels. He would remain at Nylstrom and return to Zak with the monthly caravan which traded between these two places. I personally was unimpressed with our guide who had the cold eyes, pointed head, and thick lips endemic to his race and who was, moreover, like all his fellows, completely without a sense of humour.

Uniquely, however, he spoke perfect English and a smattering of the desert tongues in addition to his own language, so he was obviously a valuable addition to the expedition. To my regret, however, Scarsdale said that he would be travelling in our tractor for the first day. Scarsdale had a habit, when we were under way,

of dividing his time between the tractors; in that way he could
see how each of us handled the machines and, what was more
important from his point of view, discover how we dealt with the
various emergencies that inevitably came up during the course of
each day. So I was relieved to know that the formidable figure of
the Professor would also be aboard; I should have all my time fully
occupied in controlling the machine and I did not relish the somewhat malignant figure of the dwarf hovering over my shoulder
during all of the difficult day.

It was a morning of shouting wind and brilliant sunshine,
the second week in September, when we left Zak; the Mir had
graciously consented to see us off in formal style and I took photographs of him shaking hands with Scarsdale and Van Damm and
otherwise recorded the historic moment for posterity. The sullen
people of the city, as was their habit, showed as little enthusiasm
for the occasion as they had for our coming and there were only
about a couple of dozen people, mostly officials and administrators from the Palace staff, who had come to salute us into the
unknown.

They stood in a semi-circle as the whine of the tractor's motors
cut through the noise of the wind, and raised their strange, three-
pronged wands of office in grave farewell. Van Damm's vehicle,
with pennants bravely fluttering, was first off, though this was
merely a piece of show. As soon as we were under way my tractor,
which would carry the guide, would be in the lead position and the
others would take station on us. In the meantime the dwarf Zalor
pointed out the general direction to Van Damm; we were heading
south, but would have to shift and tack across the great sand wil-
derness to avoid certain geological features.

At last, with the other three great machines lumbering across
the ridge and making for the distant point where the earth ran out
into browny-grey sand, Scarsdale stood on the steps of Number 1
Command vehicle and waved a dignified farewell. I recorded the
moment for the official archives and then turned to follow him
into the machine; Zalor was in front of me and he missed his foot-
ing on the shallow metal steps. Something tinkled down to his
feet. I bent to the ground and picked it up and handed it back to

him. His dark eyes looked malignly at me and he thrust the article
back into the pocket of his blouse without a word.

I went to my padded leather seat and waited for the Professor's
instructions; he was already on the radio to the other vehicles we
could see as faint clouds of dust about a mile ahead of us. The air
was full of static and muttered instructions. Zalor came and stood
by the chart-table and conferred with Scarsdale.

The Professor touched me on the shoulder and I looked up at
the illuminated map on the bulkhead which showed our progress
as a tracing. Zalor was turning the repeater arrow to put my compass on course. I noted due north and my true course and pulled
at the levers to incline the tractor blades in the right plane. Scarsdale switched on the powerful electric motors and nodded to me. I
put the machine in gear and with a barely perceptible shudder the
tracks were engaged and we were off. Dust blew about and I could
see in the panoramic rear mirror the Mir and his party slowly dis-
appearing as though a sponge of sandy particles had wiped them
away.

Then we were crawling over a slight ridge and the towers of
Zak were lost over the horizon. Far ahead the three clouds of dust
that were our companions dipped and wallowed like ships at sea
as they tried conclusions with the first wavelets of the vast sea
of sand on which we would shortly be embarked. I adjusted my
gloves, braced myself in my leather armchair and brought the two
compass needles in line as Scarsdale set the true course.

I was so busy I hardly had time to think about the article the
dwarf had dropped before we set off. Though he had almost
snatched it from me in his haste to secrete it back on his person
I could hardly have failed to realise its significance. It was nothing
more than a square fragment of ancient stone. A type of stone
with which I was becoming familiar. It bore the faintly obscene
hieroglyphs found on the Patterson Expedition to the Arctic and
on which the Professor had spent such detailed study over the past
few years.

Six

I

Dust obscured the windscreen as I settled Number 1 on course and we passed the other three machines, which fell obediently into line astern. It would be tedious to relate all the incidents of the next days; days of hellish heat and sand; of lurching misery within the tractors. Yet despite all the difficulties – we retired to rest every night at the early hour of nine p.m., completely exhausted after a day spent controlling the bucking, pitching vehicles – we completed the two hundred kilometres of baking desert within four days, a tribute to the design of the machines.

Both Scarsdale and Dr Van Damm were delighted with the performance of the tractors and though one of the spare machines piloted by Prescott had given some trouble necessitating changing the bearings on the main tracks, all four vehicles arrived safely at Nylstrom on the evening of the fourth day. Zalor, though my suspicions of him had hardened if anything, had proved a good guide, navigating unerringly, even in the middle of swirling sandstorms which added to our discomfort.

Every night we camped on the most level terrain we could find, the tractors drawn up in a hollow square to keep off the icy wind which sprang up with the advent of sunset. We could not have fires – there was no fuel with which to ply them – so two large types of primus stove developed by Scarsdale were brought into use. These served the dual purpose of heating our little party and brewing our tea and other small luxuries, and though we enjoyed the social occasion of this hour after sunset, the gritty sand which flew about took away what small pleasure the picnic had given and after that first evening we took to gathering within Scarsdale's command tractor for the communal meal, before dispersing to our beds for the night.

Zalor, for some reason best known to himself, did not like the tractors when at rest, though he was comfortable enough when they were mobile, and wrapping himself in his cloak slept under the command vehicle, in a sort of nest he scratched for himself in the sand. This suited me perfectly and the first evening I locked the door after him, content in knowing that he would be spending the following day in Van Damm's vehicle. The doctor would be leading and all I need do was follow in his wake.

I had long debated with myself the secret knowledge of the tablet the dwarf bore within his robe; he himself had never so much as referred to it by word or sign after that first moment on the tractor steps. I felt I ought to discuss it with Scarsdale at the earliest opportunity yet at the same time I feared any disruption it might bring to our little band. After all, there might be some perfectly ordinary explanation; perhaps the Professor himself had given him the tablet to assist in his guiding the party.

And yet, as I lay comfortably on my bunk, listening to the gritty sand dashing with low clicks against the windscreen glass, backgrounded by the moaning sigh of the wind as it gusted at the corners of the vehicle, I could not bring myself to broach the subject and during the day there never seemed the opportunity. As though by tacit agreement the Professor himself was now no longer communicative; he lay on his own bunk opposite, a great steaming metal mug of tea at his elbow and pored over voluminous pencilled notes he had made in a tattered exercise book.

Every now and again he would refer to sets of figures he had inked on a small chart he kept pinned during the day to the navigation table and his mumbled calculations sometimes went on into the small hours. The tiny circle of luminosity thrown by the chart-table lamp, which he kept directed on to his bunk for this purpose, outlined his beard with golden light and the long wisps of steam ascending towards the lamp from his untasted tea made a homely touch in the remote spot in which we found ourselves.

This was the image, the last thing usually noted before sleep, which stayed with me and haunts me still in the long reaches of the night in these wretched after-years. As late as his figures kept him, Scarsdale was usually the first abroad in the early morning. We were astir before six a.m., in order to catch the cooler hours of the day – the desert was a furnace by nine o'clock – and the Professor made himself unpopular every morning around six by operating the klaxon on the front of our vehicle, which must have stirred the echoes for miles around.

We usually ate our breakfast – made from tins and packets – while we were under way and the Professor took over the controls from me for half an hour to enable me to eat each morning; this was a blessed relief and I spent the time at the chart-table looking at the strange lunar scenery ahead, which was a unique experience for me, as I usually steered by the compass bearing and had little time to note the more subtle gradations of landscape.

Indeed, this would have been difficult in any case, as I was no longer leading and Scarsdale was at this time swinging the tractor wildly, following Van Damm's dust. All the while we progressed, the rim of the dark mountains on the horizon slowly climbed up the sky.

The desert seemed devoid of life of any sort and the only figures we ever saw were near dusk on the afternoon of the second day; the outlines of three tattered nomads on a distant billow of sand who regarded us as though we were carven images on some distant tomb of ancient Karnak. I know not why such a conception flowed into my mind but this desert, though it is nothing like that of Egypt, ancient or modern, could not help reminding me of that younger civilisation.

I say younger advisedly for the region into which we were penetrating in such an erratic but remorseless manner was infinitely older and more blasphemous. I think we all sensed that after our arrival at Nylstrom, on the evening of the fourth day. I do not know what we had expected; Scarsdale, of course, had been there before and the town was no surprise to him. I am selecting my words imprecisely here because town was hardly the one to describe Nylstrom, which was nothing more than a huddled collection of baked-brick hovels, divided into three or four rectangular streets, with a small brackish lake and a few miserably stunted trees which were, however, such a rarity in this area that they appeared to stand out on the horizon from a long way off. The contrast with the splendours of Zak were so marked that I felt a sinking of the heart as we came within view of this abominable village which seemed to crouch like the refuse flung down at the skirts of the mountains which now loured gigantically in the middle distance before us.

Strangely enough the people, though gaunt and sallow and much given to eye-disease, were far more friendly and forthcoming than those of Zak; paradoxically, they would have greatly appreciated the splendours of the latter city while the Mir and his followers, I reflected, with their mean and withdrawn natures, should have inhabited Nylstrom, which was all they deserved. I was standing at the door of the tractor a few minutes after our arrival, surveying the busy crowd which had gathered in the wretched town square to welcome us, and my thoughts must have been transparently obvious on my features for the dwarf Zalor, squeezing past me in the dusk, turned to give me a look of hatred over his shoulder and hissed something in his unintelligible, broken-tongued language.

Though I detested the fellow, I must admit that he had done his job well and he had brought us here safely and with the least waste of time. Scarsdale, of course, was on familiar ground again and I could see his huge figure bobbing about the crowd and now and again he paused to shake hands with someone he recognised from his earlier expedition. I was still of two minds regarding Zalor's stone tablet but the events of the next few hours and our settling in at Nylstrom temporarily banished the incident from my mind. We had a brief conference over supper in the command tractor that evening; Scarsdale told us we would be in Nylstrom only two days before setting out on the last stage of our journey to the Black Mountains.

This was the first time he had used the correct topographical title for this group and we all looked at him with interest as though we were about to hear major revelations, but he did not let drop any further information that evening. He did say, however, that we would leave Number 4 tractor in reserve at Nylstrom and proceed with the other three, which would make things much easier. There was just time, on our arrival, in the last light of the fading sun, to stroll to the edge of the village to glimpse what we would be facing. The Black Mountains were only a bare fifty miles from us now and the going promised to be easier.

There was merely a flat plain of black volcanic ash and the scouring winds which blew continually from off the mountains raised a low, fog-like cloud which would cause some discomfort. But the compensating factor was that the temperature was lower here and we would not have to endure such heat as we had encountered in the desert. Prescott and Van Damm accompanied me on the walk; our other two companions were with the excited crowds in the square. Zalor had disappeared somewhere on an errand of his own.

The view was both bizarre and magnificent. The wind had temporarily dropped and the shifting storms were subsiding; through the unearthly veil they drew over the Plain of Darkness the sun shone in carmine splendour, staining the distant tops of the blunt-spiked mountains until it seemed as though the whole of the far horizon were a mass of shimmering blood. Across the face of the mountain mass were striated white lines which looked, at that distance, like nothing so much as an intricately traced map or, if one were particularly fanciful, the many-stranded structure of a spider's web.

Even the normally icy-tempered Van Damm seemed affected, for he gave a low, muttered exclamation under his breath, the gist of which I did not catch.

"I wish I had brought along my camera," I exclaimed involuntarily. "This would make a splendid subject for the film introduction to the final approach."

The doctor shook his head.

"You are young, Plowright," he said slowly. "I don't like it. I don't like it at all."

And he turned his back resolutely on that scene of brooding splendour and neither would he enlarge on his remarks at all, though I several times returned to it that evening.

All he would say at a later stage was, "There is northern blood in my veins, some generations removed, Plowright. The northern races are, as you know, mystics. The Black Mountains as a geographic conception on the map are splendid. Seen as a reality they arouse in me feelings which you, as an extremely young man from my standpoint of years, could hardly be expected to share. I pray that you do not come round to my way of thinking before this trip is over."

2

I retired to bed somewhat irritated and puzzled at Van Damm's attitude. The whole idea of the Great Northern Expedition was, from the layman's point of view, extraordinary; when we set off four out of five did not know exactly where we were going, except that it was opposite to north. And until now Scarsdale, though he had given many hints and spoken to me personally of shifting lights and writing on stones, had only spoken practically of rubber boats, tractors and of the importance of having some people of physical strength along.

But my mind thrives on enigmas and if the truth were told most of my adventurings had been along these lines; I neither knew nor cared where my journeyings took me, providing that I could be free to take pictures and that I had agreeable companions with whom to share the journey. And this great enterprise promised abundance of both. Pondering on this and various other things I fell into a broken sleep.

I woke round about three a.m.; though we had the tractor shutters closed I knew that it was before dawn. I lay awake for several minutes before checking the time by my illuminated wristlet watch. What had aroused me was a minute, metallic noise; a noise which was presently, and furtively repeated.

I opened my eyes fully at this point and by slightly turning my head I was able to bring the Professor's bunk into focus; his large bulk was impassive beneath the blankets, the faint respiration of his breathing clearly audible. He was fast asleep. I turned my head slowly away from him when I became aware of a blurred shape sliding across my field of vision. A minute breeze blew into the closely regulated temperature of the tractor interior; someone had opened the outer door of the command tractor. A moment later it shut with a click which was the replica of the one which had originally awakened me.

It sounded once again as someone tested the handle from outside. I was up and groping for my trousers by this time; I swiftly put them on over my pyjamas and put my bare feet into my slippers. I saw a shadow pass across the windscreen of the tractor as I was doing this. It had gone to the left so I waited a few seconds before I myself opened the door and slipped quietly out into the night.

We had parked the machines in a small cul-de-sac by some metal-beaters' workshops just off the main square of the town, so I knew my quarry could only have gone into the square. I felt fairly confident of picking him up again. I was fairly certain also that I knew who he was. None of our colleagues were likely to visit the command tractor at night and leave again in such a furtive manner. I had picked up a strong leather camel whip, a gift from the Mir of Zak to Scarsdale, from the chart-table and I flexed it meaningfully as I crouched for a moment, adjusting my eyes to the light.

When I gained the edge of the square I found I could see some distance ahead and I had no difficulty in making out the hunched figure of the dwarf Zalor which flitted ahead of me over the atrocious surface of the rutted plaza. I knew his destination now and I slackened my pace and skirted round the edge of the square, keeping watch from a sort of arcade of roughly fashioned stone which fronted some craftsmen's stalls.

Earlier that evening Scarsdale had decided to overhaul our equipment before we set out for the last stage of our journey to the Black Mountains. For this purpose he felt it would be an easier proposition if we dismantled as much material as possible that night in preparation for the work the following day. Accordingly, we had taken motor drive units, radio sets and many of the working parts which made the tractors operational out of the machines and placed them in a store-room which the people of Nylstrom had made available to us.

The headman or whatever he called himself had secured the whole place with a wooden bar and Scarsdale himself had sealed the room with a chain and padlock out of the expedition's stores. I now knew why Zalor had paid us a visit; he was after Scarsdale's keys. The store, which normally housed vegetables and dried herbs grown by the people of Nylstrom was only in a small court giving off the other side of the square, so there was no need for me to hurry, as I was certain of Zalor's destination.

I kept watch, therefore, until he had disappeared in the misty light and followed on at my leisure, giving him a minute or two to release the padlock from the rough wooden door. I wanted to be certain of his malignant intent before apprising Scarsdale of the dwarf's perfidy. I stopped again when I reached the opening through which my quarry had disappeared and waited. It was a fine, dry night, though quite cold and I shivered a little as the wind probed at the thin material of my pyjama jacket. The night invested the humble buildings of Nylstrom with a majesty they notably lacked by day and from far off, though it could not be all that far, owing to the town's geographical compactness, a stray dog howled in a hungry fashion.

I could now hear a furtive chinking up ahead and once a small electric torch flashed; I smiled to myself in the gloom. No doubt Zalor had been at the expedition's stores too. He had been carrying on his shoulder what looked like a canvas bag, when I had last sighted him in the square, and I felt certain he contemplated flight after some mischief against us. There was nothing moving in all the night and no-one stirring in any of the dingy buildings in the locality but I felt somewhere out there the brooding presence of the Black Mountains, which were almost a palpable reality, even in the darkness.

There was a grating noise as I still hesitated and then a muffled thump. That would be the lowering of the bar from the door. I crouched low and eased myself round the corner, careful not to make my presence known. I still wanted to give Zalor a last chance to prove his innocence of motive and if I revealed myself beforehand, he would be able to fabricate some quite innocuous reason for his presence in that place and at that time of the morning.

The grating noise continued and then the dim light of the torch disappeared within the vegetable store. I crept noiselessly towards the light and after a few moments found myself in front of the building. Zalor had drawn back only one half of the double portal, no doubt to shield the light from the outside, and I stood behind it to conceal myself. I need not have worried about such precautions; the man inside the store was far too preoccupied with his own affairs to have any time for further concealment.

He was now acting with a reckless disregard for noise and I could hear the swishing sound of straw being raked about; I peered round the edge of the rough timber door. Zalor had placed his torch on one of our generator casings so that its light shone on the floor and walls before him. All our equipment was stacked around in preparation for tomorrow's work; as I watched, Zalor completed piling the straw around it and scuttled to the far corner. He came back with a squat green can, which I recognised. It contained paraffin, of which we had quite a store in case of emergency, or for use in lamps if we were operating away from the tractors.

I did not need to wait any longer. The matchbox fell from Zalor's hand as I sent him sprawling in the fury of my first rush. He was up again quickly though, hissing something in that abominable language of his. I got in two good blows across his shoulders with the leather camel whip I had brought with me, I am glad to say, and the pig-like screams with which he greeted my ministrations were extremely satisfactory to me. He was a powerful fellow, though, despite his small stature and he closed with me fiercely, clutching at a curved-bladed knife he plucked from his belt.

I had dropped the whip in my anxiety to hold his knife-hand off and he got his boot up into my groin while I was doing this; a stabbing pain lanced through me, the room grew dim and I fell back against some boxes. He rushed at me again with the knife but cracked his knees against some low piece of metal equipment chance had left in that spot and collapsed with a howl. By this time I had got to my feet and who knows what would have happened had I not heard Scarsdale's welcome voice shouting from the square.

The dwarf hesitated, thrust his knife back into his belt with a garbled cry of hatred and was then gone through the door and into the night. I got to my feet and half-dragged myself to the door before I collapsed again. I must have presented a sorry sight, panting, covered with dirt and straw and gasping out an incoherent story as the gigantic form of the Professor loomed up in the dim glow of the torch.

He gripped me by the hand, his jaw tightening as he looked around the room. He led me to sit on one of the upturned crates and stopped my broken flow of words.

"On the contrary, my dear Plowright, you did extremely well," he said. "If these had been burned the Great Northern Expedition would have been finished. The fault is mine. I should have foreseen something like this and mounted a guard."

The occasion was so unusual and the friendship between the Professor and myself so close at this moment that I told him about the stone tablet I had seen the dwarf drop. He was silent for a long moment.

"It makes no matter, Plowright," he said. "We have both perhaps been a little remiss but the major responsibility must be mine."

"But what does all this mean?" I asked him.

"I should have mounted a guard," Scarsdale said softly, as though he had not heard my question. "Can you walk all right? We must tell the others and make sure there are no further inter-ruptions tonight."

He had locked up again and we were halfway across the square before I was able to repeat my question.

"There are those who do not wish us to find the resting place of the Old Ones," Scarsdale said sombrely. "Zalor was obviously of them or in their employ."

We were at the tractor by this time and he paused at the door as I prepared to go in.

"I must have words with the Mir about this on our return," he said grimly.

I went inside and brewed some tea for all of us, waiting for the running footsteps and excited questions Scarsdale's errand would arouse. There was no more sleep for me that night. When I had carried the urn of tea to the vegetable store where my colleagues were already servicing the equipment by the light of portable gen-erating equipment, I went to drink mine by the edge of the town, looking over the Plain of Darkness; there was nothing to see but I knew that the sun would eventually arise from that direction.

I wondered whether Zalor was somewhere out there or if he had fled back in the direction of the ancient City of Zak. I won-

dered too how he would survive, or whether he had friends among
the desert tribes. I smiled grimly to myself in the darkness. People
like Zalor always survived. The headman, hastily roused by Scarsdale, had a party searching Nylstrom street by street but I guessed
the dwarf would have his plans laid too well and that he would no
longer be within the town. And so it proved when dawn eventually
came.

Long before that I stirred to find Van Damm by my side. He
joined me in my vigil until the distant rays of yellow light harshly
illuminated the black plain of ash before us; the dawn wind sent
faint whorls of dust moving uneasily on its surface. We looked in
vain for any trace of Zalor.

Van Damm glanced at me sombrely. His face was haggard in
the strange light of that ancient place.

"A bad business, Plowright," he said. "And an ill omen for this
enterprise, I fear."

Seven

I

The command tractor shifted and lurched on the Plain of Darkness,
the immediate foreground of the windshield filled with whirling
dust and cinders. I could see the Black Mountains rising from the
raging dustclouds like some monstrous whale-like creature, they
were so close. Scarsdale was silent at my side, now peering anx-
iously ahead, now making abstruse calculations with his slide-rule
and mathematical instruments on the chart-table before him.

I went back to steering on a compass bearing, conscious that in
a little more than an hour we should be off the plain and into the
foothills of the Mountains; Scarsdale had told us that there was
some vegetation and we intended to follow up a shallow valley
which eventually rose steeply and would take us to our destination. I only hoped the tractors would be robust enough to raise
us on to the plateau which would lead us to the cave formations
of which the Professor held such high hopes. Once again I mar-

velled at his tremendous vitality and strength in undertaking such a colossal journey on foot and with such an ill-equipped expedition as the earlier one.

When the excitement over Zalor's treachery had died away in Nylstrom and all the Headman's searches had failed to discover the dwarf within the town, Scarsdale had held a brief council of war. We had decided to press on to the object of our journey as soon as possible. To that end the technicians among us had proceeded with the overhaul of the tractors and Number 4 had been left in the vegetable store, padlocked and under day and night guard. I was set to boiling water for the tanks of the three remaining vehicles, for that would be our biggest lack once we were among the mountains. I also took charge of gathering what fresh vegetables and fruit there was available, which would make a welcome change from the material in our tinned supply.

From the night of my fight with Zalor, Scarsdale had insisted on breaking out the weapons and we all wore sidearms; some, in addition carried rifles. I found the heavy pistol strapped to my waist in its webbing holster a tremendous nuisance and I had very little idea how to use it so that I felt I should be a greater danger to my companions in an emergency, rather than to any supposed enemy.

I took a last group of still photographs of our helpful Headman and his people; and staged the few cinema shots necessary for this section of the route. I had stayed behind to record the scene as the villagers waved off the three remaining tractors into the unknown distances of the Plain of Darkness and once I had stopped the whirring motor of my machine and carried it and the heavy tripod off across the desert to where Scarsdale had halted to pick me up, I could not help reflecting on the contrast this scene would make with that of the splendour of the departure from Zak; the Plain was doubly sombre in the light of our later knowledge.

The Professor and I continued in Number 1 Command vehicle, with Van Damm alone in the middle and with Prescott and Holden in the third vehicle at the rear. Scarsdale had hoped to cross the plain in four hours or so at our maximum cruising speed but in the event it was nearer six before I heard his warning mutter; I altered my steering vector and the tractor's treads grated over solid rock as we slid upwards out of the warm dust and into the welcome shade of some stunted trees. A stiff breeze was blowing down the gully and when I had steered the tractor about a mile down the arid draw in which we found ourselves, the Professor decided to make camp. The sun was already low in the sky but as it now set from us across beyond distant Nylstrom, our shadows were long on the ground before us and the dark replicas of our strange vehicles were stencilled on the rocky floor of the valley as we pulled the machines into a rough circle and cut the motors.

2

For two days we followed the winding contours of the valley, every hour rising higher and higher into the mountain range, whose arms almost imperceptibly and inevitably closed in behind us until we all had the feeling that we were in a giant's grip. The wind increased daily, blowing in gusts from the heart of the range, but it did not trouble us as the desert wind, as there was little dust to obscure our view. It did, however, add to the difficulties of steering and our vehicles tended to yaw from side to side so that one wearied at the handles and muscles craved relief from the buffeting, which went on hour after hour.

It was growing steadily colder too, though the sun shone as regularly as hitherto; this did not bother us at first but we were then aware, during our frequent halts, that the breeze was a chilly one and we were beginning to feel the benefit of the sheepskin-lined coats which was one of Scarsdale's strange-seeming requisitions for the expedition's stores. The way twisted and wound upwards and for most of the time we were steering the tractors at half-speed through mazes of gigantic boulders and among formations of weirdly striated rock.

But there had been no major difficulties; the tractors were standing up well to the wear and tear of this difficult going and, most important of all, there had so far been no impossible places; no doubt due to Scarsdale's detailed surveying of the route on his previous journeyings. If there had been one impassable section

then that would have made the Expedition untenable; apart from
our using the tractors as mobile bases, there was the sheer impossibility of transporting the masses of stores and equipment along
these miles of pitiless moraine. The territory through which we
were advancing was quite featureless; black rock; boulders; stunted
trees; above, a perpetually blue sky; ahead the eternal probe of the
restless wind in one's teeth and the jumble of rocks which indicated the next bend.

We were too close in now to see what peaks lay ahead and so
far as one was aware we were not high enough for snow. Scarsdale
still continued in his mysterious and inscrutable way. Though his
charts, log books and tables of weird hieroglyphs multiplied on the
chart-table in the command vehicle at night, he gave no detailed
hints of what we might soon expect.

We had been several days on our journey to the plateau when I
myself broached the matter one evening; he shook his head, with
an enigmatic smile.

"We are not close enough yet," was all he would say. "Time
enough when we are within the Galleries."

He had with him a translation of the blasphemous book, The
Ethics of Ygor, which had been typed on ordinary foolscap sheets
and he would be lost for hours in its study most evenings, the
smoke from his pipe curling upwards vertically in the still air of
the tractor. While in the desert we had kept within the machines
whenever we stopped. There was good reason for this, of course;
the tractors were air-conditioned and the sand and grit constantly
blown about made eating and conversation in the open air a
misery.

But here just the opposite rule obtained. Though the air was
cold and the wind blew chill, whenever Scarsdale called a halt over
his radio link and all three vehicles drew into a rough laager, we all
of us, without anyone ever putting it into words, foregathered in
the open air, lit fires and cooked our food. Huddled in our sheep-
skin jackets and hoarding our precious gatherings of wood we
drank our nightly tea-ration and made the mountains echo with
our animated talk.

Van Damm in particular made his own attitude plain; I could

read it well enough on his face, though he never put the feeling into words. We were whistling in the dark, his taut features said to me every night, as he gazed apprehensively around him at the dark rock whose jumbled surface was lit by the flickering flames of our necessarily feeble fires. We all felt it now; the mountains were closing in on us and inside the tractors the feeling was only emphasised. When we were asleep this did not matter; but until then we preferred to chat among ourselves; lounge outside; braving the wind, downing the hot sweet tea in thirsty gulps and constantly scanning what little we could see of our surroundings. But I noticed that none of us strayed outside the triangle of tractors, in which the fires formed the cheerful focal points. So far as we knew there was no wild-life in the mountains and no dangerous crevasses into which we might fall; but still we did not wander.

Day was a different matter but even there I noticed my companions rarely ventured more than a hundred yards or so from our established camp. The only exception was Scarsdale; he was, of course, as I knew, absolutely fearless and sometimes at night he would disappear for as long as half an hour at a time, on some mysterious expedition of his own. On the first occasion this happened I was consumed with alarm and was about to call my companions when he emerged from the darkness, the small round glow of his pipe illuminating his bearded features. His notebook was in his hand and there was an excited look in his eyes, but I had learned my lesson by now and I did not venture to question him.

But I remembered that he had traversed this way alone and with none of the advantages that we five currently enjoyed and once more I marvelled at the tenacity and endurance of the man; he had moral integrity as well as physical endurance and there were times as the weeks lengthened, that I came near to adulation of our leader. The Great Northern Expedition was certainly the highest point in my wanderings in a life not entirely devoted to mundane things, and even though the Professor's purposes remained shrouded in obscurity I felt I would have followed him almost anywhere he chose to lead us.

We were four days traversing the gulley; towards the end the scree and the shattered boulders which lay like great shards of rock fallen from a region as remote as the moon, made progress maddeningly slow. But the tractors behaved extraordinarily well; I think each of us, underneath, harboured a fear that the motors of the machines might overheat or that breakage of vital components would strand us here. For that reason those of us who were driving nursed the vehicles along.

It was unlikely, I reasoned, that all three of the machines would break down, but stranger things had happened; I cast my mind back to my own adventures in the Arizona Desert and Crosby Patterson's terrible and unique fate and pictured what might happen to us were we thrown on our own resources and have to return on foot. That outcome was unthinkable and I preferred instead to concentrate on my immediate duties.

I was pleased, during the second day, when Scarsdale announced to me that he would himself take over the controls of the command tractor. This left me free for other duties, not least those of my photographic recording activities and I secured one of the best sequences of the entire movie record the following afternoon, with my series of swooping pans and tracking shots from the windows of our vehicle, as we crawled inexorably into the higher plateau of the Black Mountains.

It was a fearsome landscape into which we were slowly edging our way and Scarsdale had still not revealed to us our exact destination or what our role would be; he sat now, bracing himself in the padded seat, his great hands firm and steady on the levers, gently coaxing the power under his hands. The command vehicle would shudder, hang sickeningly on the edge of some unseen rock shelf and then with a lurching motion, step quietly into a higher plane and then proceed again smoothly enough until the next obstacle was met.

The mountain walls ahead now completely blotted out the sky and for the last day or so the sun had disappeared; everything around us was in purple shadow and then we came out again round a shoulder of hill and a high sun, spilling in from behind us somewhere cast a pallid glimmer on the blackness of the shoulder of mountain beyond. Nowhere was there any sparkle of light or any relief in the sombre shade of these oppressive peaks; the wind still blew steadily but seemed to have lost some of its sting and the noise of our motors thrown back from the rocky walls each side of us seemed less sacrilegous.

On the afternoon of the final day the grating noise beneath the tractors' treads finally ceased and we lurched along in an odd silence; it was near lunch-time when this happened and Scarsdale gave the order over the radio for the party to halt for the break. I was down and out of the cabin door almost before we had stopped and I gave an exclamation. Scarsdale joined me at the door, with an amused expression in his eyes.

I then saw the reason for the unexpected silence. Stretching behind us, like the slime-track left by a gigantic slug was our own trail, every scratch and indentation on the tractor treads reproduced exactly on the surface of the gulley. I printed my own foot-marks behind me as I ran back towards Van Damm's tractor, which was just turning the bend. The entire floor of the valley was lined with black sand, a unique and extraordinary sight; if it had not been for the perennial blue of the sky above us the effect would have been overwhelming in its morbid darkness.

Like an engraving to illustrate the stories of Poe or a work by Doré or Samuel Palmer, the Black Mountains literally ingested us; they were above, behind and before us and now their own ebony opaqueness stretched beneath our feet. Van Damm had joined me and then the others; the tractors were formed into the familiar triangle and we all stood about, talking little, overcome by this bitter darkness which blackened our very spirits. Only Scarsdale seemed unmoved; in fact his demeanour was positively jaunty under the circumstances and he gave out at great length over our al fresco lunch on the nearness of our destination and the positive tasks on which we would shortly be engaged.

We were under way again within the hour and the soft crunching of our progress along this dark sea of sand combined with the whine of the motors to lull my mind into a semblance of rest. The far-off rays of the sun had disappeared behind the far hills long ago but the light in the sky was still brilliant when I looked through the windscreen and saw that the way before us was at last blocked.

Darkness stretched supreme from the black floor of sand to the

dizzy heights of the mountain peak far above us; Scarsdale drove
the tractor onwards, over a hummocked ridge, where the sand lay
in strange whorls like the casts of crabs, presumably sculptured
by the wind. I got out the tractor. The sand terrace sloped away
from me gently towards the face of the cliff; darkness married with
darkness in the gigantic face of rock before me.

The echo of something like great wings broke the silence as
the other two tractors whined to a halt, our companions leaping
to the ground. I found a crack in the rock formation with my eye,
followed it up to misty heights like a Gothic cathedral. A huge
shard of rock breaking out of the sea of sombre sand shocked
with its pallidity. I walked over to it. The rock, white and crystal-
line like quartz, shone like a blasphemy in that place of shadows.
My suddenly shaking hand traced out the outlines of strange and
obscenely-shaped hieroglyphs upon it. It seemed to point like a
finger towards the entrance which beckoned before us. I turned to
look again as Scarsdale walked towards me.

A warm wind blew out of the cliff and with it the memories
and associations of something far off and long ago. My eyes raked
the cliff again, refusing to believe what they saw. A hewn doorway in the black basaltic surface of the natural rock. A doorway
that seemed to lead to the utmost depths of the earth. A doorway,
moreover, that must have been all of five hundred feet high.

Eight

I

Aeons seemed to pass as we gazed silently at that stupendous
entrance. My soul was completely overwhelmed at the sight and
I could not, did not in fact, dare contemplate what manner of
being could have used such a doorway in the dawn of time. Unless
the construction had a purely symbolic significance. To cover my
confusion I returned to the Command tractor and sought my photographic equipment; the photographs I busied myself taking were
excuse enough not to engage in speculation with my companions.

Scarsdale was the only person who did not seem overwhelmed by the sight before us. He stood with his legs apart and his arms folded across his massive chest and gazed before him as though he were in the tranquil atmosphere of one of the London or American museums; in his eyes was an infinite satisfaction and I realised that this moment represented a culmination of his life's work. In one way his entire career had been an advancement towards this point. The others recognised it too, and kept apart from the Professor, the small knot they made clustered in front of the gigantic entrance symbolising their puny stature by comparison with this freak of architecture.

I finished my moving picture work and picked up my still camera again; I was setting up my tripod to take close-ups of the hieroglyph inscriptions on the stone when a shadow fell across the pale surface of the obelisk. I turned, expecting Van Damm, but it was the Professor. He gazed without saying anything, while I completed my exposures. I turned back to him when I had dismantled my equipment. His lips were moving noiselessly as he traced the carvings on the stone with his fingers. He seemed almost oblivious of my presence.

"Let he who will, enter," he said, like a man who was choosing his words with care. He knotted his brows together and tried again, stumbling over the phrases.

"Let he who enters, remain," he continued. Van Damm had joined him by this time and watched the performance with grim concentration.

"He who remains will not return," the Professor concluded. He made some notes in his book.

"I didn't know you were able to decipher the inscriptions, Professor," I ventured.

Scarsdale looked at me with thinly disguised triumph. "I have been working long years at this, my dear Plowright," he said. "These carvings are hardly unfamiliar to me. And I had The Ethics of Ygor to guide me."

"Hardly an inviting message for such an entrance," said Van Damm with a return to his old waspish manner. He looked an oddly enigmatic figure as he stood in his old cord riding breeches, legs in brown leather boots straddling the sand.

"I do not think we need worry overmuch," said Scarsdale comfortably. "The Old Ones were inclined perhaps to exaggerate. You forget that I have been here before."

"And you returned safely," I put in. The tension seemed to lift as I said this. We had been joined by the other two now and we all stood in a small group round the Professor, like students at a site lecture. Which is exactly how I felt. All these men had greater knowledge than I as to why we were here and Van Damm and Scarsdale were two of the foremost authorities in their own fields.

"Perhaps the Old Ones wanted the Professor to return," said Van Damm softly. "He is, in effect, drawing others in."

Scarsdale smiled. "You have too much imagination for a man of science, doctor," he told his tall colleague. "I have, as Plowright so aptly observed, returned to tell the story. Not without difficulties, as you all know. But my struggles were against physical obstacles only. There is nothing within the caverns that would lead me to believe they support any form of life inimical to man."

"That may be because you did not penetrate far enough, Scarsdale," said Van Damm calmly. "The Trone-Tables speak of the guardians and there are other, certain indications, possibly more forbidding . . ."

"This is no time to discuss it," Scarsdale broke in authoritatively. "It will be dark in an hour or two and we have much to do. We camp here tonight and tomorrow we leave Number 3 tractor as a reserve inside the entrance. From then on we travel in two machines only, in constant radio contact. You will command Number 2 Van Damm, as hitherto and I Number 1. We will take it in turns to lead."

Van Damm nodded and the small group broke up, its members walking back towards the tractors. Their footprints made disturbing trails in the dark sand behind them.

I lingered for a moment, looking for a lens-cap which had somehow escaped its cord and fallen to the ground. As I found it and replaced it on the camera I was startled to hear again something I had heard before, echoing from the darkness beyond the lintel of the great door. It sounded like the distant beating of gigantic leathery wings.

2

Curiously enough, that evening saw a reversal of our usual practice regarding the camp sites. It may perhaps have been the brooding atmosphere of the great entrance in front of the mountain; or possibly the connotations of the message on the massive stone obelisk but without anyone saying anything specific those of us who were driving the tractors formed them into the familiar triangular pattern on the sand outside, well before darkness fell.

Neither was there the usual camp-fire gathering. Instead, we all foregathered in Scarsdale's Command tractor for a rather special meal. Holden, who was acting as cook on this occasion, excelled himself in preparing the tinned delicacies and Scarsdale himself even went so far as to break out three bottles of champagne from our precious reserve store.

He did another strange thing also; there were, in the roofs of the tractors, special skylights of toughened glass, which were protected inside and out by heavy steel shutters, controlled electrically. I had never seen these in use during training in Surrey or in the field, but tonight, moved by some whim, the Professor drew back the shutters. The brilliance of the stars overhead illuminated the interior of the vehicle and Van Damm moved to the control panel, clicking switch after switch, until all the interior lights were off.

The faint luminosity from outside grew in strength until it seemed to us as though the starlight were bright enough to read by; we must have made a strange sight, sitting in that pale glow, sipping champagne, the only other sources of light the minute radiance given off by the Professor's pipe and by the tip of Van Damm's celebratory cigar.

Then, after half an hour of this, Scarsdale got up to trip the light switches and the shutters rumbled back across the skylight. The atmosphere grew brisker. The Professor gave us a final briefing; he urged caution on the morrow and reiterated his instructions on the importance of the radio link. He reminded us too that we should be using the searchlights on the tractors under field conditions for the first time.

He himself had charted the way on his previous journey and he anticipated no difficulties during the first days; we would wear light clothing as the caves and passages were warm and dry. We would carry sidearms at all times and no-one was to leave a vehicle without specific permission from him as leader of the expedition. All this was sensible enough and yet I felt a faint unease as he continued his discourse, his strong face outlined in the glow from the Command vehicle's instrument panel. I thought again of the leathery flapping I fancied I had twice heard from within the cave entrance. I wondered, not for the first time, what were the Professor's reasons for taking along so many heavy weapons. Looking round at the racks of equipment and lethal arms in the interior of the tractor, I reflected that we seemed more like a band of mercenaries invading a fairly weak nation, than scientists bound on an archaeological field expedition. It was a feeling which persisted long after the start of our journey the following day.

I slept badly this last night. I drifted off to sleep on each occasion, only to awake an hour or so later, my mind vaguely troubled. The last time I looked at the illuminated dial of my watch to discover that it was only a quarter to four in the morning. A sudden scraping noise jarred my nerves; the bright yellow of Scarsdale's match threw a glow over the whole interior of the tractor. He puffed irritably at his pipe for a moment or two, his strong features beneath the beard looking like the image of some old Nordic god. It was a comforting sight before it died, leaving only the faint glow of burning tobacco.

I heard the rustle of blankets as Scarsdale put his matchbox down somewhere on his bedding.

"Are you awake, Plowright?"

It was a statement not a question.

I admitted that I was.

"You are worried about the coming operations?"

The word had slipped out; once more the activities of the expedition had assumed those of a military adventure, rather than that of a strictly scientific affair.

"Only inasmuch as your true purposes are obscure to me, Professor," I said. "I have every confidence in your abilities both as a man and as a scientist, if that has any value to you."

"Thank you, Plowright," said Scarsdale. "It is true that I have been perhaps a little lax in not preparing you more fully for what we may find. But that is only because I myself am not certain. Most of my reasons exist as mere theories in my notebooks. I would prefer to measure them against actual experience in the field."

"I quite understand," I said. "Please do not think I am complaining."

I found myself searching for the right words. The Professor said nothing but emboldened by the steady and comforting glow of his pipe in the darkness, I went on.

"I must admit the size of that doorway and the somewhat forbidding inscription on the stone had a certain effect on my mind," I told him. "But you'll not find me wanting if we run into any difficulties on this trip."

"I never doubted it, my dear Plowright," the Professor said. "That was one of the major reasons for your selection. But you have other reservations? Your tone seemed to imply it."

"They're perhaps too intangible to qualify," I said hesitantly.

"Would you care to trust them to plain speech?" the Professor said, with a return to something of the manner he had maintained when we were training in Surrey.

"Fancies, perhaps," I said. "I am possibly over-imaginative where such places as this are involved. Your models, the caves and the other details you gave us in the original briefing were among my major reasons for coming along. Imagination's my strong suit, as you may well know and I certainly need it for my photography and artistic work."

"And you felt the Great Northern Expedition would give you such scope in your capacity as cinematographer and official cameraman?" he concluded for me.

"Something like that," I admitted.

The Professor was silent for a long moment and then I heard the soft click as he put the dashboard panel lights on; their blue dimness outlined the details of the cabin.

"But you now feel that your imagination may be a handicap once we get underground?" he continued.

"It may be," I said. "Though we shall be within the tractors most of the time. I have been underground before, of course, but it's not just that. There's something different about this trip and not only from what you've said, though that was bizarre enough."

"Would you care to give me a concrete example," he asked.

I hesitated for another long moment. Then I told him about my feeling at the entrance of the cave.

"Ah, then you heard it too," he said sharply. "I wondered at the time. Yes, it was very like the beating of wings, as you say. Bats, perhaps."

We did not return to the matter again and in a few moments more we slept. But within I did not think the noise I had heard had been made by bats and I could swear that the Professor did not think so either.

Nine

I

The honour of being the first one within the great portal was given to Holden; I say honour, such as it was, because the event, like most long-awaited incidents, was almost an anti-climax. We were awake and out early next morning and soon after six a.m. the three tractors affronted the morning air with their motors. What little sun there was penetrated our dank spit of dark sand reluctantly and its gilt was soon lost again against the black, basaltic rock which seemed to absorb light and somehow stain it. The simile is fanciful, I know, but the only one that readily springs to mind.

Holden drove the tractor across past the obelisk and into the cave-mouth where the machine was rapidly lost to sight; Scarsdale was already alongside the entrance and followed him in on foot. We waited for perhaps ten minutes and then both men appeared; Holden re-joined Van Damm in Number 2 tractor and Scarsdale assumed command of Number 1. He put the key of Number 3 vehicle into a drawer in the chart-table; we would pick up the spare vehicle on the way back.

I looked out through the windscreen; Van Damm's machine was describing a circle, ready to fall in behind us and the tinny static of the radio receiver in our cabin was already alive with the doctor's waspish injunctions.

"I will take over the controls, Plowright, if you please," said Scarsdale. "I know the route, as you realise and I shall need you to control the radio and searchlights. We shall carry out the same routine we have regularly practised."

As he spoke I was already vacating my padded chair at the chart-table; to be perfectly candid, I welcomed the arrangement because the radio and other work was nominal, whereas the control of the tractor was exacting, both physically and mentally and likely to be difficult within the winding caverns of which Scarsdale had so often spoken. Besides, I hoped to do some photographic work with the special fast film I had brought along, if Scarsdale's lighting units permitted.

I acknowledged Van Damm's perfunctory verbal message and thanked him for the formal good wishes to Scarsdale for the success of the enterprise. Scarsdale could, of course, hear perfectly well what was being said via the monitor speaker mounted on the bulkhead over the chart-table and he gave an irascible snort at what he considered to be Van Damm's excessive formality. I left the switch at the open position, for that was the instruction, and I should also have to relay back to Van Damm any special orders relating to obstacles we might meet en route.

I ran my eyes over the lighting switchboard and then looked ahead as the massive portal of the huge doorway loomed in front, the lintel lost to sight high above. In the steel rear mirror I could see Van Damm's machine, pennants fluttering, skirting the obelisk; then we were within the cave mouth and the darkness reached out to embrace us like a cloak. A warm wind blew from the interior of the earth – we had the air vents open and I could feel this – and the whine of the motors echoed back shrilly within the cave walls.

The noise died as Scarsdale reached forward and cut off the air vents from the outside; at the same moment the light of the sky faded to a feeble yellow. At a nod from Scarsdale I switched on the main searchlight, which was mounted in a nacelle above the tractor windscreen and could be swivelled by a control from within the machine. The yellow incandescence, with which we were all to become so familiar, outlined the faint contours of a rocky wall which was lost as it curved upwards into a blackness darker than any night known to outer earth. Shadows fled fantastically across the middle distance and I was momentarily startled to see a vast fluttering until I realised it was our own image thrown upon the tunnel by the searchlight of Van Damm's vehicle behind. I looked briefly in the mirror to see that he had taken station about thirty feet back and acknowledged his movement by using my microphone.

Holden replied laconically; I concentrated ahead and saw that Scarsdale was following the tracks of Number 3 tractor. We saw it a moment or two later, parked up against the right-hand side of the tunnel wall, where it bulged out to make a natural bay. We did not stop but drove straight on, only virgin sand before us now. The tunnel was about thirty feet wide here and it was not to vary much for the next few hours; I had already switched on our measuring instrument so that we could keep a constant check on the miles we covered each day.

I reached for my camera and as Scarsdale grimly concentrated on his steering, I briefly put on all the lighting equipment we possessed; the effect was startling and I busied myself in taking several photographs, both front and rear, before switching down again to the main searchlight only. I had noticed something however, that raised a number of startling conjectures in my mind. Firstly, the roof did not, as is usual in cave formations, come down fairly close to the ground at any point.

The second detail which struck me was that the corridor of stone stretched monotonously ahead for perhaps half a mile and did not vary greatly in its width. The floor also was no longer composed of sand but seemed to be made of rock. This heightened the noise levels within the tunnel considerably, though it made little difference to the comfort and stability of our ride within the tractor. The thing which impressed me most of all, however, was the regularity of the cave walls; before an hour had gone by I had become convinced that the tunnel was not a natural formation at all but had been engineered at some distance remote in time. This raised in its turn a number of fascinating conjectures because I had formed the impression that the inscriptions on the obelisk and the portals of the great doorway were of great antiquity. The engineering problems involved in the vast tunnel along which we were now travelling so smoothly and with as much facility as one would in a modern city's underground system, would have been incredibly complex and difficult without modern machinery and tools. There was a stupefying engineering talent at work here greater than that of the Incas and the Mayans and incomparably older, if what Scarsdale had said was true, and an excitement similar to that which must have animated the Professor in his long years of research and study on the project, began also to animate my own mind.

This must have occurred to Van Damm at almost the precise moment because his high fluting voice came through the loudspeaker, asking to speak to Scarsdale. I told him that was impossible for the moment, as the Professor was at the controls. There was a brief lull, broken only by the crackle of the instrument.

"You have noticed, I take it, the regular conformation of the walls of the tunnel, Plowright," he began.

"The implications had not escaped me, doctor," I said.

Scarsdale smiled quietly to himself at the controls.

"Would you please ask the Doctor to maintain radio silence except in emergency," he said. "There will be time for discussion and examination of the tunnels when we stop for lunch."

I conveyed the Professor's message to Van Damm in a more diplomatic manner and with that he had to be content. We drove along the seemingly endless tunnel for several miles; once I went to the rear of the tractor and read off the mileage indicator. Already it registered fifteen. I told Scarsdale and he merely nodded in a satisfied manner; it was obvious that he knew our destination. His confidence at the controls was masterly and it was uncanny to see the way he almost foresaw any slight shift in our direction; the wind continued to blow steadily and warmly, as I regularly noted by opening the vents. Although the compass needle swung quite broadly on the shallow curves we were sometimes encountering, we were steadily heading almost due north. Eventually, if the Professor's scale models in the far-off study in Surrey were accurate, we should be at an enormous distance beneath the earth. There had been no calls from Van Damm's machine during the remainder of the morning, though the radio switches remained open, but I could see that they were keeping pace with us effortlessly; both tractors were doing a steady ten miles an hour and there was little or no dust beneath the treads to obliterate the view. I was keeping the log this morning and I entered all these details at fifteen minute intervals, to Scarsdale's evident satisfaction. I asked if I might take over the tractor and give him a rest but he shook his head.

"After lunch will be time enough," he said. "Compared with the desert this is an extremely comfortable morning's drive."

We exchanged no further words and I packed up my photographic equipment, my mind completely at rest for the first time since we began our field operations. We were going slightly uphill, I indicated in my last log entry of the morning, made just before our first break at 12.15 p.m. The mileage indicator, allowing for a pace that varied between five and ten miles an hour, indicated an awesome 55 miles beneath the surface of the mountains.

2

We did not spend much time within the tractors at lunch-time; the two machines were set up side by side and with the main searchlights illuminating the camping area and the tunnel ahead of us. It was a bare, antiseptic atmosphere; the floor, of hard whitish rock, was dry and free of insect or any other type of life that we could see. The walls bore the marks of ancient cutting tools of a type I had never seen before; Van Damm and the others were somewhat excitedly conferring with Scarsdale and I wandered at will, taking pictures and thinking of the people who could have built upon this terrifying scale. I had tilted one of the searchlights upwards toward the roof but despite its power I could not find its limits; there was nothing but inky darkness above and no sign of any bat or bird-life. There would have been an awesome silence that I would have found personally hard to bear, had it not been for the warm and steady breeze that blew from somewhere far off down the tunnel. Altogether, it was a strange, and fascinating place in which we found ourselves.

Geoffrey Prescott and Norman Holden both had an air of barely suppressed excitement, a sort of bubbling effervescence just below the surface, that came through even from under the façade of strictly impersonal scientific materialism which they carried about with them. Like the rest of us, they had now donned light overalls and the alloy helmets which Scarsdale had developed and which were meant to guard us against falling rocks.

This headgear, which bore stencilled numbers, from Scarsdale's appropriate One down to my humble Five, also incorporated powerful flashlights which we found extremely useful, as the light in such a position left our hands free to carry tools and equipment. Both Holden and Prescott carried notebooks and jotted down data, conferring among themselves, as they hurried here and there along the tunnel.

"It conforms fairly closely to your sketches and models, Scarsdale," Van Damm told the Professor as I wandered close to them. "Are there any places where the tunnel splits up into tributaries?"

"Only just this side of the water," Scarsdale said shortly. "We'll have to leave the machines there and take to the boats. I don't, of course, know what formations we shall find on the other shore. It is perhaps fortunate that there aren't many choices; we could spend years exploring blind alleys, otherwise."

Van Damm cleared his throat. "I have noted the marker posts of which you spoke. They would appear to correspond to measurements of ten of our miles."

The Professor smiled, his face enigmatic in the yellow incandescence of the searchlights.

"I had cause to note them on foot," he said. "An experience, I can assure you."

"How long did it take, Professor?" I asked.

Scarsdale turned his great bearded head toward me in the harsh glare of the lamps.

"I calculated, afterwards, over a fortnight," he said sombrely. "The worst part was the darkness. I had only a couple of electric torches and some candles, and these had to be conserved. In the end I navigated by using my walking stick against the tunnel wall, much as a blind man might do. I calculated I wore nearly a quarter of an inch off the metal ferrule."

I could not resist a shudder at the Professor's words and I thought again of the fantastic will inside the hard exterior which had kept him going along these miles of sinister corridors when lesser men might well have been reduced to gibbering idiocy by the darkness and the loneliness.

"You had a compass, I take it?" said Van Damm softly, after a along silence.

"Thank God," said Scarsdale. "One becomes completely disorientated. It might be thought a simple matter; right-hand wall going in, say; left-hand going out. But right is left and left is right in the darkness, if you see what I mean. North going in and south going out was the only way, allowing for slight deviations where the tunnel curves."

I walked on down the tunnel, the faint throbbing of the searchlight generators from the tractors coming over the faint sighing of the wind; the black walls stretched on without a fleck of discolouration or a glimmer of any variation to break their monotony. It was an artery of darkness leading to utter stygian blackness; a man on his own could quickly degenerate to madness in a place like this. I felt for one moment that even without lighting one would still be able to discern the blackness of the tunnel walls. That was the impression the place had on one.

I halted abruptly in my perambulations and came quickly back at this point. There came the tapping of a hammer up ahead; Holden was taking a sample of the rock floor. He swore mildly as I joined him; I looked down and saw that the head of the hammer had snapped from its stout wooden handle. Scarsdale smiled grimly.

"You won't have much luck there, Holden," he said. "This material's harder than granite."

"That's what worries me, Professor," said Geoffrey Prescott. "How the hell did these people work such material? And, for all that we're talking about thousands of years remote in time, they must have had more sophisticated tools than we've been able to develop."

"I have my theories about that also," said Scarsdale cryptically.

I noticed then that he kept his hand near the revolver strapped to his belt. And I noticed also that a light machine-gun on its stand had been brought out from Number 1 Command tractor, presumably by the Professor while we were finishing lunch. Its workmanlike barrel pointed straight down the tunnel ahead of us.

Ten

I

We were rumbling slowly ahead again in the inky darkness, our speed reduced to a mere crawl, the searchlight probing the monotonous miles before us. I was steering now, while the Professor sat brooding at the chart-table, every once in a while pausing to stare out of the windscreen; he remained fixed in his attitude for perhaps a quarter of an hour on these occasions and I wondered again what calculations were being evolved within that massive cranium.

Scarsdale had told us we would conserve power in the reduction of speed and though we remained in constant radio contact this first day, I myself thought that Scarsdale hoped to alleviate the monotony of the journey; in truth the somewhat boring and fatiguing routine involved in making the long preliminary approach to the object of our search left one inordinately tired and debilitated. But I noted that Scarsdale's concentration did not relax for one moment and I realised also something of the reasons for the change of driver in Number 1 vehicle and the slackening of speed.

The Professor sat in his padded leather seat behind the chart-table and occasionally would interrupt his calculations to pick up the night-glasses which stood at his elbow and scan the tunnel ahead as though by this he would bring our destination nearer. We had been travelling for more than two hours in this way; the warm air blowing steadily through the vents; the whine of the motors making a repetitive fugue in one's ears; the compass needle swinging ever so slightly with the minute variations in the direction of the tunnel, so accurate were these ancient engineers; and the high falsetto of Van Damm occasionally piercing the static from the radio monitor on the bulkhead.

Occasionally too, there were strange variations in the rhythm of our motors and several times I had let the head of the tractor lurch round a little as I struck curious areas of shadow against the rocky wall of the tunnel; Scarsdale's muttered comments were hardly needed but the effect was annoying and made steering more difficult. I glanced in the rear mirror more than once and realised that a malicious corner of my soul was pleased to note that whoever was driving Van Damm's vehicle was not finding things any easier.

And then there came to me in detail the model in Scarsdale's far-off study among the misty hills of Surrey and I found many questions blurting to my tongue. The Professor heard me out in amused silence.

"I was wondering when you would notice," he said at length. "The patches of shadow you see are arcades leading to what other caverns and labyrinths God knows. It would take a lifetime to explore them all."

I was silent for a moment while I absorbed this information.

"You explored some on foot?" I ventured at length.

Scarsdale nodded, his eyes scanning the tunnel ahead.

"I reeled off twine and took a torch but it was hopeless. They were terrifying places. I had a thousand yards of twine and gave up when that ran out. One could wander for years out there, if the hundreds of side tunnels I came across were as extensive."

I found the implications of the Professor's remarks difficult to take in.

"Then this may be considered a city, with the tunnel its main artery," I said.

Scarsdale nodded. "Excellent, Plowright," he said. "I had come to much the same conclusion myself."

He turned to face me in the bluish gloom of the control chamber. "We have not, of course, had an opportunity thus far to make detailed observations on foot, but there were curious symbols placed at intersections and cross-over points in the tunnels. These, which were strangely incised and high upon the walls, combined with the lack of any observable arrangements for lighting the tunnels – such as torches or brazier fires – led me to believe that the former inhabitants of this place were blind and crept about the passages by feel."

The Professor's words and the circumstances under which they were uttered had such unpleasant connotations that I fear Number 1 vehicle gave a great lurch which, however, I had started to correct before the Professor's admonition. Such a supposition had not occurred to me and gave rise to such a vivid range of images that I later came to regret the Professor's uncalled-for confidence. I was even, in rather a cowardly fashion, glad that Van Damm's vehicle was to lead the following day, when we hoped to be approaching the underground lake of which Scarsdale had spoken.

We had not planned a very long run that afternoon as we wished to make rather more elaborate arrangements for camping that night. We could not, of course, have fires, even if there had been any driftwood and there was no point in being "outside" the tractors, when we had their security for sleeping arrangements. I had saved a sandwich from the lunch-break, as I had eaten little due to the excitement engendered by our surroundings, and I juggled the controls precariously as I munched at the tinned ham, occasionally fortifying myself from the thermos-flask of hot tea with which we always provided ourselves each morning at breakfast.

The Professor, when he was not studying the tunnel ahead, was busy on the chart-table with some of his more cryptic books and documents. I noticed once again his typed copy of the ancient and blasphemous Ethics of Ygor and the highly abstruse calculations which Van Damm had referred to as the Trone-Tables. His use of these ciphers and the other media with which the chart-table was strewn were far beyond my knowledge of such things but possibly the Professor had chosen me as his companion in the tractor precisely because I had the layman's mind and he could occasionally put his thoughts into words and test my sometimes banal reactions. With Van Damm he would, more often as not, have engaged in verbal battle in which these two highly trained minds were fairly evenly matched.

Now he sat with his leather-padded sleeves firmly resting on the table, his great shoulders hunched as he studied the figures before him, occasionally shaking his head as though exasperated beyond measure. Finally, he put his pencil from him and sat up in his chair, swivelling it to face me.

"I think we might as well call it a day, Plowright," he said. "You must find this tiring and after all, you have done most of the donkey work so far."

I cast a quick look at the mileage indicator; I shook my head wonderingly as I saw that the day's total – even allowing for our snail's progress this afternoon – registered no less than seventy-one miles. I mentally calculated that the longest street in the world – reputedly in Russia – could have been put down in our tunnel nine or ten times over before it would make an equivalent distance. I simply could not imagine the sophisticated engineering and equipment which would be needed to create such artefacts in the dawn of time and I put further banal self-questioning from me, as Scarsdale spoke again.

"Please give the signal."

The electric klaxon on top of the tractor blared with heart-stopping raucousness within the tunnel as I pressed the button; Scarsdale would insist on its use as the halt signal either on the surface or under the earth and I myself felt it was something we could do without as the radio link would have been just as effective. But it was Scarsdale's expedition and he made the procedure a rule so we said nothing. Holden's voice came over the radio monitor a few seconds later.

"Executive signal received. What are your instructions?"

"We shall be camping for the night in five minutes," Scarsdale replied. "Please make all necessary preparations." The black walls of the tunnel, with an occasional mouth debouching from it, continued to slide by in the yellow glare of our searchlights; already, it seemed as though we had been travelling due north for days. Scarsdale smiled wryly as I observed to him that the Expedition's title was perhaps a little more apposite than hitherto. The warm wind blew as strongly as ever, though fortunately it was still nothing more than a breeze; the air was dry; and the rock grated beneath the rustling tread of the tractors.

Scarsdale was already moving about the cabin, tripping switches which set generators re-charging batteries; testing circuits; and doing the other mundane things on which our survival depended, such as checking levels in the fresh-water tanks and preparing materials for the evening meal, which we would take some time after six o'clock.

2

I throttled back the motors, my forearms trembling slightly as they were wont to do, after some time spent at the levers, my legs aching from the transmission of the tread movements to the accelerator pedals. Sophisticated as these great machines were, and as cunningly as Scarsdale and Van Damm had designed the transmission mechanisms, they were undoubtedly tiring to drive though the going in these tunnels (I persisted in referring to the broad highways along which we were travelling in the plural) was nowhere as difficult as it had been across the desert.

But there we had the sweet sky above us, and not this lunar blackness which seemed to depress one's spirits beyond measure, even though we had been travelling under the mountains for less than a day; and to recall we had thought the desert sky cruel! I jerked out of my reverie at a sudden exclamation from Scarsdale. He was standing in a stiff attitude in front of the windscreen, his actions arrested in process of tripping one of the switches. The incident was so unusual for him that I might have been more star-tled than I seemed but I had already begun the stopping procedure of the tractor, so I merely continued with my routine.

The treads rotated ever slower and the shrill whine died away to a miniscule ticking; I switched off then and became aware of the faint respiration of the warm breeze which set up a soft susur-rance as of distant surf within the tunnel.

The motor of Van Damm's machine impinged itself upon my consciousness and I turned to see Number 2 stopping behind us; the searchlight on the roof blossomed brighter and several secondary lights came on. By this time I had joined Scarsdale at the windscreen.

"Is there anything wrong?" I asked.

Scarsdale relaxed his tense attitude. He turned towards me and concluded his switching movements on the panel.

"I don't know, Plowright," he said slowly, his face stern in the yellow atmosphere of the searchlights. "I fancied I saw something white flicker up ahead in the tunnel."

"A pity you didn't warn me," I said without thinking. "We could have run on a few hundred yards."

"That's just what one doesn't do under these circumstances," said Scarsdale, as though he were explaining something elementary to a child. "We don't know what we may meet in these tunnels. One notes; one consolidates; and one then reconnoitres in strength – suitably armed."

Here he slapped the webbing holster at his belt with significance.

"I'm sorry, Professor," I said contritely. "I didn't think."

"It's all right," he returned. "But I've naturally given this a great deal of thought over the years. And I've worked out a routine for every eventuality – I trust."

Sparks of humour glinted in his eyes as he opened the door of the Command tractor and stepped down on to the iron-hard floor of the tunnel. Van Damm had opened the door of his own machine before it had stopped and, stepping delicately on to the metal casing which protected the treads, dropped to the ground. The two men met midway between the machines and conferred quietly.

Van Damm went back to Number 2. I heard his shouted instructions, distorted between the walls of the tunnel.

"Bring the tractor up level with the other. We want to get maximum illumination ahead. Scarsdale's spotted something down the tunnel."

I stood aside as Holden manoeuvred the big machine alongside our own; when he had switched off the motors the throb of generators echoed back along the passage and then all the main lighting of the tractor came on. I went to stand with Scarsdale to one side; the grotesque shadows of myself and the Professor sprawled ahead of us along the floor. The beams of both tractors stretched a long way and I fancied I could see something faintly white in the far distance.

When I had indicated this to the Professor he called Van Damm over and the lighting of Number 2 vehicle was switched off. The five of us then conferred briefly; Holden went into Number 1 tractor and turned off everything except the main searchlight. I noticed that Scarsdale had his revolver out and the others appeared to be bristling with weapons. Even Van Damm was waving a dangerous-looking automatic pistol as he conversed with the Professor.

Reluctantly, I got out my own revolver and released the safety catch though I felt that the Professor and his companions were in far greater danger from my own incompetent marksmanship than they might be from anything in front of us.

Scarsdale turned back to me when he had finished talking to the doctor.

"You had better come with me, Plowright," he said. "We'll keep abreast. In case of emergency this will obviate anything ricochetting off the tunnel walls and injuring one of us."

I hadn't thought of that and gratefully fell in step with his burly figure as we walked away from the tractors into the encompassing gloom. Both of us had switched on the lamps incorporated in our helmets and the bobbing shadows which flickered and flared on the walls either side the farther we got from the comforting beam of the searchlight, made a weird pattern that formed a fitting accompaniment to my sombre thoughts.

We had now got more than two hundred yards from the tractors and were passing the dark mouths of various archways; these were no doubt the side tunnels to which Scarsdale had already referred and I hoped they were as empty as my companion supposed. We could easily be cut off from the main body if anything in this labyrinth wished us harm. I wondered whether the Professor had thought of this but I hesitated to mention it, in case he might find me over fanciful.

I felt my arm silently gripped and at the same time I saw what the Professor wished to draw to my attention; the flicker of white I had glimpsed from the distance was markedly nearer and with every rasping footstep we took began to resolve itself from the gloom. Presently, in the manner in which the image of a developing photograph composes itself before one in the developing tray, we saw what was undoubtedly a human figure lying on the floor of the tunnel.

Scarsdale steadied his revolver and his face was stern in the light of our head-lamps. He tightened his grip on my arm.

"Stay here," he said quietly.

"Ought I not to go with you?" I queried. "In case of danger . . ."

"In case of danger one alone will be enough," he said firmly. "You can do more to help by staying here. In emergency you would be able to do a great deal more to help me."

I saw the sense of this and said nothing further. There ensued a long thirty seconds as I stood and watched Scarsdale's lamp bobbing and dwindling up the tunnel before me. The rasping of his footsteps ceased and there was just enough light to see that the Professor was kneeling to examine something. He returned a few moments later, walking backwards down the tunnel towards me, fanning his revolver from side to side.

He stood next to me and took a deep breath.

"It's the dwarf, Zalor," he said in a rather unsteady voice. "Though God knows how he could have got here. He's quite dead. We'll bring the machines up and dispose of him."

The next few minutes were a confusion of tractor motors, dipping lights and anxious questions. Holden went out with Scarsdale to drag Zalor into one of the side tunnels. I could confirm that it was he from this nearer view and I recognised the clothing he had been wearing. He looked curiously deflated as I gazed at his remains from a distance; Scarsdale would not let anyone else approach closer.

He and Holden went out later and while they were away I went back into Number 1 tractor and brewed some much-welcomed tea. When I went outside again Scarsdale gave the order to back the tractors down the tunnel and make camp there. I noticed that one searchlight was kept on; Scarsdale ordered permanent sentries to keep watch throughout the night and one of the light machine guns was set up on top of the Command tractor and an extension wire to the alarm klaxon run out for the sentry's use should it be needed during the night.

I viewed all these precautions with disquiet which was not alleviated by Holden's behaviour; he had apparently been taken sick, said Van Damm, who had attended him. Holden did indeed have several vomiting attacks and when I offered him tea later he had a face that looked ashen and haggard. He took the tea sullenly, quite unlike his usual self and sipped it with great shuddering gasps between.

Scarsdale also looked more grim than I had yet seen him and often turned his night glasses down the far curve of the tunnel, towards the side entrance where they had taken the dwarf's body. No-one slept much that night and towards midnight I found myself in conversation with Holden in Number 2 vehicle. He looked better than he had that afternoon but his eyes had a strange, haunted look which I didn't like. As we talked – myself interrogatively, he in brief, disjointed monosyllables – his eyes wandered ever and again back to the windscreen of the tractor and the dark bend of the tunnel in the far distance, cut off where the tractor searchlight beam's power failed to penetrate.

"It wasn't so much the loss of weight," he told me finally, "though that was bad enough. The dwarf was like a husk from which all the essence had been drained."

Holden cast a curious look over his shoulder, at the tunnel beyond the windshield.

"All his face seemed to have been sucked away," he said, the greyness back in his own features. "I ask you, what sort of creature can have done that?"

It was a question which made sleep impossible for me also that night.

Eleven

We made an early start next morning. It had been a wretched night, not improved by a false alarm from Holden during the small hours when he fancied he had seen a shadow moving farther down the tunnel. Fortunately he had not fired, as he might well have injured himself with the ricochet but the infernal noise of the klaxon which tumbled us from broken sleep, and the equally noisy inquest which followed, made rest for the remaining hours impossible. By five we were moving forward again, myself at the controls of Number 1 which, despite his previous instructions, the Professor had insisted should lead.

It was a position of honour, as Van Damm had said, but I could not help wishing as I juggled with the steering handles, that Number 2 had gone ahead as planned, as the lead under our present conditions was a far from relaxing station. It did not seem to worry Scarsdale who kept his night-glasses rigidly inclined through the windshield and occasionally gave me instructions to reduce or increase speed. Van Damm's voice came through on the radio at ten minute intervals and to outward purposes all was as it had been the previous day; but there had been a subtle change with the finding of Zalor's body and for myself I knew that I could never again regard these tunnels in quite the same way.

They had always been sinister – I was conscious of that the first instant the tractor rumbled beneath the great portico – but the knowledge that we had also now to deal with some force inimical to life charged every foot of the way with unknown terror. It could not be ruled out, however, that Zalor had been the victim of some quite natural disaster; a beast of the order of a mountain lion, which perhaps inhabited the deepest caverns? But even as Van Damm put forward the supposition my own secret voices were mocking the theory; on what would living creatures of that sort subsist in these arid tunnels? And surely we should have seen some evidence of them long before now?

Beasts leave droppings or some other signs of their passing, but there had been no evidence of life of any sort. And then there was Holden's reaction; given that he might well have a nature particularly sensitive to death but Zalor's end had been so horrible that Holden had, for a time, been almost out of his mind; and even Scarsdale's grim resolve had been shaken. There remained other problems also; not least the puzzle of how the dwarf had managed to cover such a vast distance to arrive at the caves before the expedition. Or had he perhaps companions at Nylstrom who had carried him with them across the desert more swiftly than our tractors could travel?

There were endless possibilities here and my mind revolved them equally endlessly; the truth was that the alternatives were so disquieting that I was determined to find a natural explanation, however bizarre, which could be made to fit. In the meantime my hands automatically carried out their tasks; the wind blew with increasing warmth; and the needle of the compass pointed obstinately almost due north.

But we were not to travel very far today before a major landmark was reached; it was something after seven a.m. and the mileage indicator registered, I think, around eighty-four miles before I began to sense a slight change in the atmosphere. It was nothing immediately definable but I was conscious that Scarsdale had noted it also. I saw that he had his head cocked on one side, as though he were listening. But I noticed, a short while later, that he was not listening but looking at something. It was quite five minutes more, however, before I myself became aware of the phenomena which had arrested his attention.

This was mainly due to two factors; one, the position of the searchlight which reflected back a steady glow from the rocky walls of the corridor; and my own position, down below the chart-table where the upper edge of the windscreen prevented me from seeing the object of the Professor's curiosity. But as we progressed towards our eighty-fifth mile beneath the mountains there could no longer be any doubt. It was growing lighter.

2

We were five miles in depth below the mountain tops, according to Scarsdale's calculations and yet a form of twilight existed which made the full-time use of the searchlights unnecessary. We had now almost reached the ultimate point of the Professor's original exploration and from now on we would all be traversing unknown territory. The light underground at this point seemed to emanate from some phosphorescent source high up in the impenetrable fastness of the roof.

Curiously, it appeared directed entirely downwards, instead of at the sides of the tunnel so that the source of the illumination and the structure and height of the roof itself remained hidden. The light was bluish in tinting and gave a corpse-like pallor to the objects beneath and to our own faces, but it was a relief to be no longer within the stygian blackness through which we seemed to have been moving so long.

The light grew in strength, but at no time did it become strong enough to approximate to what we called earth-light – that is, ordinary daylight above – and at its greatest intensity resembled that of dusk in the tropics in the few moments before the sun disappears below the horizon. Nevertheless, it was a great boon to be able to move about and to perceive objects from a distance.

A short while after I was able to steer the tractor visually from surrounding observations, we came out from the tunnel and the vibrations which had been accompanying us for the past two days, died away. We were running on something which felt like and resembled the black sand in the mountain gorge. As soon as this occurred, Scarsdale called a halt, the searchlights were switched off and we all got out the tractors.

It was an extraordinary sight; we were in a vast cavern lit by the flickering, ghostly blue light which made the far distance shimmer and undulate. We appeared to be on a wide shore composed of the dark sand and a shingle-like substance, which grated beneath our feet. The light seemed to come from a "sky" far above our heads but which Scarsdale explained was emanating from the phosphorescence in the roof of the cavern at a vast distance above us; this was the reason why we were still unable to see the limit of the gigantic geological formation which formed the cave.

We stayed near the tunnel entrance for about half an hour while my companions took measurements and navigational positions while I tried, possibly unsuccessfully, to capture something of the scene on film; the tunnel entrance into the vast cave was quite small at this point and appeared to be the only means of entry. The chisel-like marks on the engineered wall just ended, as though the tunnellers had got tired of their immense task and the surface of the cave interior was of natural rock.

I found myself next to Van Damm as we all wandered around, marvelling at the strange quality of the shimmering light.

"What I can't understand, doctor," I said to Van Damm, "is how this ancient people realised they would come to this cavern."

Van Damm smiled. "Rather ask yourself, Plowright, whether the people who inhabited this cavern were not more concerned with breaking out and drilling a communication tunnel through the mountains to the open air and the valley beyond."

The explanation was so simple and logical that I must have looked as foolish as I felt for Van Damm burst into a short, barking laugh and said, "Don't look so crest-fallen, man. Like many laymen you were merely working from the wrong premises."

He excused himself and went to consult with Scarsdale while I finished my photographic work and collected my apparatus. The wind still blew freshly from the north but now it had a more glutinous taste to it; it was difficult to describe but I felt somehow as I had once felt when taken as a child on a long-promised first trip to the seaside.

I got in the tractor to find Scarsdale already at the chart-table, making notes.

"This is a great day Plowright, is it not?" he said enthusiastically, his eyes burning in a way I had never seen before. "In a few minutes we shall be at the spot where I was finally forced to turn back. From here on in we shall be embarked upon a modern voyage of discoveries."

It was difficult not to be affected by his enthusiasm but I still had my inward misgivings; though I disguised them as best I could and went instead to the control seat and awaited his orders. I asked him what course to steer.

"North, of course," he said impatiently. Then he added, with a softening glance at me, "I'm sorry, Plowright, I'm forgetting my manners. Excitement, you know, and pressure. We've only a mile of beach to cross and then we make permanent camp."

The tractor treads bit softly into the yielding sand and the noise of the motors was now lost in the vastness of the great domed cave as we set off on the last stage of our extraordinary journey through the shimmering, misty light of that underground domain. Van Damm's machine pulled up alongside us and I saw that he had once again raised his pennants which were slightly agitated by the faint wind and that generated by the tractor's passage, which for a moment or so gave me the illusion that we were travelling in the open air.

We had now lost sight of the sides of the cave and were travelling across a wide sandy plain into a shimmering haze which obscured our vision, so that we might have been advancing toward some distant horizon. Indeed, the illusion was so complete that there were times when I completely forgot that we were not still upon the surface. Scarsdale had not forgotten our place or purpose, however, as I noticed he had his revolver out and beside him on the chart-table. Van Damm maintained the radio link and apart from our taking station abreast and the fact that we had no artificial lighting switched on, all seemed as normal as our habitual routine underground.

And yet it was not normal, could not be normal, and for the first time since we had been beneath the surface of the mountains, I began to experience a feeling of tingling excitement; I put this down to the illusion of being on the surface. Truth to tell I could not have maintained my morale had we continued much longer within the eternal darkness of the tunnel. The mileage recorder registered a little over eighty-six miles when we at last came to the extreme limit of our journey, at least so far as the tractors were concerned.

I had for some minutes been conscious of a humidity in the

atmosphere and a slight disturbance in the middle distance which resembled the lazy breathing of a restless giant. As we advanced over suddenly wet sand I then saw what appeared to be a thin line of surf which flowed and receded before us, leaving a glistening iridescence upon the sloping surface of what, for want of a better term, I will call the beach. I was already slackening the tractor's speed and at the executive signal both machines turned to port together and we drew back up the shore-line to a commanding position where the water was unlikely to penetrate.

Curiously, now that we were here Scarsdale seemed to have lost all interest in the scene before us. To my mild astonishment I heard him give radio orders to Van Damm that no-one was to leave the tractors; that as soon as engines were switched off we were to start battery re-charging procedures, clear up the interiors, check rubber boats, weapons and ammunition. Looking back now, this routine and somewhat dull programme made excellent sense. We did not know what we would be facing and there would be all the time in the world for examination of our surroundings later.

Our survival would depend upon the efficiency of our equipment and if anything happened to the tractors it seemed, despite the Professor's previous experience, unlikely that so large a party would get back on foot without some major disaster. Scarsdale was an exceptional man and one built for survival under adverse conditions, but I did not see myself as being cast from that heroic mould and the remainder of our companions, though exceptional men in their fields, were probably not of sufficient physical calibre, though these things are always difficult to ascertain with any degree of accuracy.

So we spent the remainder of the morning on our allotted tasks, without going outside and even lunched within the tractors, until our leader was satisfied that things were as far forward as they could possibly be. Then he set us all to dragging out the rubber boats, military stores and other equipment on to the foreshore; it was not until late afternoon, when we had set a guard, inflated the two large rubber boats and set up two machine-guns on tripods that he announced his plans. To our astonishment he said that it would be a further two days before we would embark upon the underground lake; he called it a lake but it was like a small tidal sea. He did not know its limits but despite the vast length of the tunnel we had traversed, he would guess it to be fairly small, even though it had a minute tidal movement. He had ascertained on his previous visit that the water was brackish and it did not seem to contain any marine life of any sort.

His plan was to continue to steer almost due north and hope to hit another beach on the far side of the lake. The party would then explore onwards, always leaving good margins for food, water and stores in order that we could return. The boats would be left on the far shore and we would then proceed with tents. The time spent at the present site, which Scarsdale had designated Camp Two, to distinguish it from the spot where we had left the reserve tractor at the tunnel entrance, would be employed in training and exploration.

As I saw it Scarsdale intended us to concentrate on our weapon training; and we would also be taught how to handle the somewhat cumbersome rubber boats, which were of bright red material, which stood out well under the dim phosphorescence of the atmosphere. We would try to explore the limits of the beach; take samples of sand, rock and water for analysis; perform life-jacket and life-saving drill; practise filling the special packs in which we would have to transport our belongings; and also pitch tents and strike camp, all things we would have to get used to on the other side of the lake.

Scarsdale, somewhat jokingly, had suggested naming the tunnel along which we had so laboriously travelled, the Van Damm Passage, in honour of our companion; the doctor had flushed scarlet at this and had stammeringly disclaimed the distinction but Scarsdale insisted on pencilling it on the large-scale maps that were being drawn by our companions. Now, as we walked briefly on our first reconnoitre towards the shore, Van Damm reciprocated by suggesting that we dub the lake the Scarsdale See, a suggestion which found favour with the whole party.

It was in this amiable state of mind that we all set to after lunch, only Prescott's movements being conscribed, as he was on the first guard-duty, having to remain by the tractors and within easy reach of the klaxon and machine-gun. The remainder of us then walked slowly down towards the water's edge, three of us at least marvelling at the unearthly vista before us. Before I describe our surroundings, one action of the Professor's drew audible comment from Holden; oblivious to the weird beauty of the scene he seated himself on a spur of black, basaltic rock which thrust itself out of the sand before us and buried himself in The Ethics of Ygor, occasionally humming to himself as he consulted his columns of figures.

We waited politely until he had finished his calculations before moving on; when he was ready Scarsdale jumped up with a muttered apology and came towards us. He then acted as our guide, setting off along the shore at a brisk pace, the rest of us falling into step. I do not think I shall ever forget the spectacle that was spread before us that afternoon, in a place which had no dawn, day, night or sunset and in which all sense of time was lost; a region of other-worldly beauty which we were forced to subordinate to our man-made notions of time, order and routine.

The first thing we noticed was that the sluggish tide which rose and fell a foot or two on the shallow shelving shore, was itself as phosphorescent as the light which came from the sky. In between was a sort of vaporous mist which hung in thin sheets over the surface of the water, so that we were able only to see about two hundred yards out from the beach, when all was lost amid the indistinct haze. But the faint luminosity of the water, the brief lacunae caused by the mist and the recurrence of the vibrating brightness from the vast roof of the cave, hidden from us, made the whole atmosphere nothing more reminiscent than some great painting of Turner, gigantically enlarged.

We walked for about a mile westwards along the beach until our passage was barred by a configuration of rocks which thrust out into the water, so sealing us off, as the landward side of the mass was sheer and unclimbable. We came back, each heavy with his own thoughts, all of us exhilarated and moved at the strangeness of our surroundings. On our return I relieved Prescott who was then free to join the others in another sweep to eastward. I remained on top of the tractor, straining my eyes until the last of my companions had dissolved into the blur of the atmosphere.

I passed a long hour and was then relieved to see the four of them returning. They had found a similar situation to that obtaining to the west. A broad beach, misty water and finally impassable rocks. Scarsdale was inclined to the theory that the rock formations were masses broken away from the main walls of the vast cavern when it had solidified in pre-historic times and the others were of similar opinion. None of them felt that the rocks had any particular significance and that if it had been possible to scale them they would have merely led the explorer, sooner or later, to the blank, impassable walls of the main cave.

From figures the Professor had worked out, based on measurements and theories expounded on his walk, he had advanced the opinion that the lake or tarn, despite its apparent tidal tendencies, would not prove to be of vast size, though he had surmised it might be a mile or more in width. We were not proposing to explore its longitudinal limits and Van Damm felt that the tide might be caused by inlets, at some vast distance beneath the earth, running down into one end of the lake and out at the other.

We debated earnestly within the tractor that evening and many were the theories that Van Damm and Scarsdale argued; it was, from my point of view, one of the most stimulating and interesting evenings we had yet spent, the burden of the earlier nights having given way to a light-hearted optimism on the part of the three junior members. Even Holden was more like his normal self, though I noticed, that, even when off watch, he cast occasional glances through the windscreen, as if to assure himself that all was well outside.

Van Damm had taken the first of the two-hour watches and was, thus, the first to observe the sheer monotony of the atmosphere here, the light never varying by the slightest degree from the overall twilight. But even this mundane fact was written up in the voluminous notebooks which the Professor and his companions were beginning to fill with columns of figures and other statistics. I took my own watch at four in the morning and though the slight breeze from the north still blew, the atmosphere was not damp as might have been supposed from the nearby presence of water; neither did I hear or see anything untoward.

Ever since the strange flapping noise I had first heard at the great portico entrance several days ago, which might now almost be measured in years so long did we seem to have been beneath the surface, my nerves had been playing me strange tricks. The horrifying and quite unexplainable death of Zalor had completed the stealthy undermining of my morale and so I faced my first turn of sentry-duty, my companions all being asleep, with rather more tension that I would have liked.

But all passed without incident as did the subsequent spells of watching over the next two days. We fired the various weapons, with differing degrees of success, the dull explosions seeming to start weird echoes from far off across the water. We hauled the rubber boats down to the edge of the brackish lake and embarked, paddling a few hundred yards out into the mist by compass, and then turning again, making our way back to the beach without mishap. The rubber lifebelts were duly inflated and each of us – not without forebodings, though the water had been already declared non-injurious to health – plunged into the cold tide until their buoyancy had been duly tested.

These, and other equally strenuous enterprises occupied us for the allotted time, until Scarsdale had professed himself satisfied with our efficiency. On the third morning, after a substantial breakfast, shortly after seven a.m. the five of us, in two rubber boats attached one to the other by the painters, slipped into the cold tide, leaving the two locked tractors shrouded under their tarpaulins, and splashed out somewhat hesitantly into the misty unknown.

Twelve

I

Scarsdale, Van Damm and Holden embarked in the first rubber boat, while Prescott and I followed. The noise of the paddles, the dripping of water, seemingly magnified by the mist and the curious pallor of the light from above made an unforgettable scene as we thrust out from the shore and were soon undulating on the choppy surface, our horizons limited by the faint mist which clung to the surface.

The rubber boats were dangerously low, we had packed so much equipment in with us and I hoped that the current would not get any stronger farther out; if we had to paddle for our lives Prescott and I were singularly ill-equipped for the task. Scarsdale's boat carried the compass and we were attached by the rope in any case so we had no navigation to do. Even so, we were hard put to it to keep up and every so often Scarsdale's sharp injunction would come across to us as the line went taut, due to our inability to match their speed.

But after half an hour Prescott and I had settled down to the stroke and our thoughts wandered in a pleasant form of euphoria, our responsibilities surrendered to those on the main craft, our minds as well at ease in this place as they would ever be. We needed both hands for the paddles, but even so our rifles were handy at our feet, wedged against crates, cases and bundles of camping equipment. My main concern had been the safety of my cameras and my supply of photographic plates; to this end I had secured them in the middle of the mound, well wrapped in waterproof material. My companions had regarded my possibly excessive precautions as faintly ludicrous and even Van Damm was tempted to remark, on embarkation, "We aren't going to America, Plowright."

"Who knows where we are going?" Scarsdale had put in unexpectedly and, on reflection, he was of course, right. The lake might be of enormous extent, if it were on the scale of the works we had already seen. My reflections were interrupted at this point by a sudden lurching movement of the craft, and its tipping at one end, accompanied by a slight ingress of water. My smothered exclamation was followed by a curt shout from the Professor and a muttered apology from Prescott, who had caught his paddle in the securing line.

The interruption was timely, however, and I looked more sharply about me, noting that the phosphorescence of the water remained unabated; that the slight tidal movement continued; and that the surface vapour had receded a little so that our two craft floated in a clear circular area about half a mile in extent. The illumination from above continued steadily so that we seemed to be sailing beneath the dim sky of earth and the warm breeze which had blown steadily from the north appeared, to my imagination at least, to be a little stronger.

With it, I fancied a faint vibration as of some great machine a long way off, giving out a pulsation like a heart-beat. I glanced at Prescott but saw that he had already heard it and looking ahead, I could see that the other party had stopped their vigorous paddling and were all poised, water running off their paddle blades in fiery particles, as they listened intently.

I was amused to see that almost immediately Van Damm bent to his knees and I then made out that he was scribbling furiously in his notebook; he glanced at his wristwatch and continued his entry as he recorded a log observation of the phenomena. After this slight pause the three paddles of our companions dipped as one and Prescott and I measured our own strokes to theirs and so the two ungainly rubber craft went bobbing and nodding into the mist.

Some fairly stiff paddling followed and from various indications, verified by Prescott, we estimated that we might be about halfway across the lake; the current strength was increasing here and it seemed to run roughly from east to west, bearing out Scarsdale's earlier theory. However, nowhere was it really troublesome and by allowing for it by heading off from true north on the compass Scarsdale and his companions ahead of us continued travelling almost due north over the ground.

It was slow work though, and we had no means of estimating our progress as we had on the tractors; without benefit of the compass and because of the encircling mist Prescott and I would have been completely lost but for the guidance of the lead craft and one could go round for hours in those conditions without navigational aids. The strangeness of the light also, both from the water as well as from what we called the sky, resulted in a peculiar sense of disorientation, and we were both glad to hear Scarsdale's hail from the lead craft about two hours later, that we were approaching the opposite shore.

At a conservative estimate we must have been covering something like three miles an hour over the ground so the extent of the
lake width might be somewhere in the region of five miles; a pro-
digious area for an underground feature of this sort. The Scarsdale
See was living up to its newly given name. Prescott and I slackened
our paddling and as we drifted farther towards Scarsdale's boat,
which had also paused in front of us, we could distinctly hear the
faint susurrance of water on the shore before us.

As we rocked slowly inwards, parallel with the first rubber boat,
I could see, from the first glimpse, that the shore was almost an
exact replica of the one we had left. Here were the same black
rocks, the water lapping at the dark sand and tumbling phosphorescent round the base of the rocks; the mist low down on the
shoreline; the dim light coming downwards through the vaporous
haze; and the sand receding into rocky distance.

I noticed that Scarsdale and our companions had their revolvers
drawn and we all waited in that uneasy surge until a gesture from
our leader set us all to paddling again, so that the two boats grated
and foamed their way ashore. We jumped on to the wet, yielding
sand and dragged the frail craft up way beyond the water line. As
before, Scarsdale was in no hurry to proceed; exploration could
wait while he established another camp and we unloaded the supplies. We chose a spot in the rear of a heaped tumble of boulders
and there set up the tents, unpacked what equipment we would
need for a night's stay and dragged up the two boats, which the
Professor insisted should be tethered to stakes driven into the sand,
though what purpose that served I did not quite see.

This was named Camp Three and the boats and the heavier
stores would remain here while the five of us, reduced to a walking
party, went on with the packs, tents and more portable supplies. But
the day's activities would include a preliminary exploration inwards
by three of the party; the remaining two would prepare the camp's
midday meal and make an effort to investigate this far shoreline
if there were time. Once again machine-guns were dragged out
and mounted on their tripods. Their line of fire commanded both
approaches to the beach, that is from west to east, but again I could
not possibly see what lay behind the Professor's reasoning.

Apart from the flapping of what I took to be wings, we had heard or seen nothing of any living creature since we went underground, though I could not deny that the dwarf's mysterious and sinister end was enough to ensure the most stringent precautions. We drew lots for the parties and it fell to Van Damm and Holden to remain in camp while Prescott and I under Scarsdale's guidance would press on to see what lay beyond the beach.

In addition to weapons we took with us a portable radio with which the Professor hoped to keep in contact with Camp Three and he also had with him a Very pistol; we were, of course, armed and at our leader's insistence we donned the headgear with the lamps, in case we had to explore any passages or tunnels away from the dim luminescence of the main caverns. Normally we would mount sentries on all our camps from now on but Scarsdale felt that as long as Van Damm and Holden kept together, they could leave camp for a trip along the beach if they wished.

Van Damm and Holden carried on unloading the remaining stores from the boats and we waited a few minutes to test the radio link before Scarsdale gave the order to start out. In single file the three of us marched up the beach; I looked back only once to see the figures of our companions already swallowed up in the haze. After a few hundred yards the noise of water ceased and the air became dry and arid; the wind blew, as it always had, from the north, that is directly in front of us and with it, for the first time, tiny particles of grit blew past our faces and lodged in our clothing.

The faint pulsations I had earlier heard were also stronger though indefinable as to source and obviously far away; we paused while the Professor noted the temperature and other atmospheric conditions in the notebook he habitually carried and I then tested the radio link again, being reassured on hearing Van Damm's squeaky voice. He also took a note of my brief report and reported in his turn that he and Holden were proceeding eastwards along the beach. They had seen and heard nothing of note. Scarsdale and Prescott had gone ahead a little by this time, but when I caught them up I passed on Van Damm's remarks, as the Professor had instructed me.

I fancied he had more confidence in me than I deserved; perhaps I gave him the appearance of being steady and reliable but my façade belied my interior. Unlike all the other expeditions on which I had engaged, the Great Northern was special in many ways, and I had rarely faced the days before me with greater foreboding. I knew that Holden had realised this also and it was my fancy that Scarsdale, for all his bluff exterior, guessed the power of the unknown forces with which we might be faced. It was true we had physically seen nothing since the expedition began but apart from Zalor there was a dreadful atmosphere emanating from this terrible twilight world that a man would have to be made of stone not to sense.

As we came up from the beach the mist had now thinned away and we were on a broad, stony gulley which stretched out in all directions before us; but our view was limited by the dimness of the light so that there was always a rim of darkness about half a mile ahead which made a natural horizon. Until we had advanced toward it we were never sure whether our way was blocked by a cliff of the black basaltic rock or the darkness was merely composed of vasty space.

We had told Van Damm we would be back in two hours, unless anything untoward occurred, which gave us an hour each way; in any case we could report any delay on the radio link. I glanced at my wristwatch and saw that we had already been walking across the plain for a little over twenty minutes. I had one of my smaller cameras slung round my neck and I stopped to set up my tripod to take a vista of the desolate scene with the minute figures of Scarsdale and Prescott now some distance ahead. I saw them quicken their steps as I was dismantling my equipment and I hurried after them just as they began to disappear into the rim of darkness.

Scarsdale, however, paused as soon as he saw that I had fallen behind and the two men waited for me to catch up; I then saw what had caused them to hurry on. There, across the plain before us, loomed a blank wall, broken by another of the gigantic portals we had already seen at the entrance to the mountain. At Scarsdale's nodded instruction I radioed Van Damm; his voice came through, after a minute or so, distorted by static. I gave him Scarsdale's message and told him to stand by.

2

The three of us then walked forward across to the great portico which loured across the plain at us. As I had surmised, there was another plinth in front of it, which bore the same strange hieroglyphs we had already noted outside the mountain range and which, according to Scarsdale, bore so sinister an inscription. I took some photographs while Prescott stood looking round in the dim light; Scarsdale had gone over to the plinth and was laboriously copying out the inscription. It seemed to correspond to some passage in the Professor's copy of The Ethics of Ygor, for I saw him excitedly comparing extracts as he scribbled. When I had finished my photographic work, I put the camera back in its case and waited with Prescott. Neither of us spoke to the other.

We went on for several minutes until the portico had grown so large that the greater part of it was now lost to us in the shimmering vastness above; the right-hand side of the massive stone blocks of which the lintel was composed, bore two lines of inscription only and I photographed these while Scarsdale again noted them. He then radioed Van Damm personally and gave him an account of our actions for the doctor's log.

As we went forward again I saw that a vast flight of steps led upwards into the gloom; the interior was not entirely dark however, and fluted openings in the roof let through the phosphorescence from above. I observed wryly to myself that we were now twice removed from the earth above and that we were plunging from the eternal twilight into the stygian abyss; I wondered how many transformations there would be, each, like a series of Chinese boxes, more subtly wrought than the last and each more irrevocably committing us to this underground cosmos with its own arid and sterile atmosphere.

As we went under the portico the Professor observed to me in level tones that we would make Camp Four just outside the entrance the following day. To my surprise the warm, dry wind still blew as we went up the stairs. These were singular indeed and took us some time to mount. Their construction seemed to be of some light-coloured stone like marble or granite; they were not worn in any way and looked as freshly-minted as the day the unknown masons had completed their work.

But the most extraordinary thing about them was their dimensions and configuration. Scarsdale's exclamation reached a climax of admiration as we went upwards and Prescott and I could not help joining in. The steps were the most remarkable I had ever seen. Each was about two feet high, so that we had to scramble awkwardly over the lip, using both our hands to get leverage; the step, if that was the right term, then ran across for more than ten feet before the next pushed upwards into the dimness, and the whole process on our part was repeated. Our progress was necessarily slow under these circumstances and as the warm wind blew steadily down towards us, I was soon perspiring fairly heavily.

Our eyes were by now used to the lower level of light inside and we did not need to use the lanterns in our helmets. I did note, however, that a narrow band of ornamentation ran along each side of the steps, separating it from the wall and I drew this to the Professor's attention. I used my head lamp for this and Scarsdale took a sketch of the zig-zag patterning which ran along the double banding of the step border. I took several pictures for the record and then we went on.

Fortunately, the flight of steps was fairly short, though of great length, due to the ten or twelve feet levels in between each one. At the top we walked forward into what looked like a long rock gallery, perfectly built, and illuminated by the fluted interstices from above. It is now the time to become perfectly precise in my description of the scene, so I must choose my words carefully. We had not gone far into the gallery before I saw that along each side were ranged hundreds of what I must call, for want of a better term, jars. They were in single file, about two feet out from each wall and each bore above it a twin-lettered symbol.

I went up close and pushed at the rim of one of the vessels; though of great thickness and weight it rocked slightly. As far as we could make out in the available light the jars were greyish in colour, about five feet high by about two feet across. They were sealed at the tops with a flat stopper of what looked like clay or rock, cemented with some mucous-like substance round the edges which caught the light of my lantern and glittered. The seal also bore hieroglyphs corresponding to those on the wall above. The sides of the jar, from the indications given at the neck were about an inch thick. They had no necks or shaping such as we understand but were merely cylindrical with a flat base and the same circumference all the way up.

Scarsdale cleared his throat which made an unpleasant rasping noise in the gloom of the gallery. The sound went echoing down the long vista and I saw Prescott visibly start and look about him. He and the Professor conferred together and presently came back to me. The Professor had a geologist's kit with him, containing various small hammers, cold chisels and other implements. He and Prescott chose tools to their liking and selecting the nearest jar, commenced to loosen its sealing stopper. Working from opposite sides, while I reinforced the available lighting from my helmet lantern, they commenced to chip away at the bonding material.

The chinking as the hammer heads descended on to the chisels stirred unnatural echoes in the gallery and once again I saw Prescott, who was staring about him as if to guard our activities from intruders, visibly wince. I could understand his feeling as the echoes seemed to vibrate down the gallery and continue long after they should have died away in the natural order of events. Of course the configuration of the gallery was probably responsible for this eccentric aural phenomena but its effect was unnerving to say the least.

The Professor and his companion worked on for several minutes and their efforts seemed to be having a visible effect; there was a steadily widening crack in the material between the neck of the jar and the sealing disc and in about a quarter of an hour the seal began to give. The Professor and Prescott then both transferred their efforts to one side, and inserting their chisels under the stopper attempted to break the final layer of coagulant material. I heard a sharp crack, a muffled exclamation from Scarsdale who had slipped over, the stopper gave suddenly and there was a rush of air or gas from within the flask accompanied by a most shocking stench which made me feel quite ill. I turned away, groping towards the steps and the entrance of the gallery.

I leaned against one of the jars to clear that loathsome odour from my nostrils. I was thus some feet away from where Prescott and Scarsdale, their activities recommenced, had lifted away the stopper. The back of Prescott was between me and the jar, with the Professor on the far side. There was a grating noise, as the vessel was lifted on to its edge and the two men started to ease something out. I heard a muffled thump, the empty jar rolled with a hollow echo to one side and Prescott gave a loud shriek which jarred my nerves.

I jumped forward, the odour momentarily forgotten, to see Prescott backing away from something on the floor of the gallery; his face was white as he turned to me and his lips moved without formulating any words. I pushed round him somewhat unceremoniously and had to bite my own tongue to prevent my cry from joining the echoes of his own.

The creature which lay before us in shimmery putrescence on the rock bed of the gallery was unlike anything in my experience. It was about four to five feet high, with a shrivelled, white maggot-like body from which depended two stringy lower limbs, hinged in three places and packed behind it. On its back were gigantic wing-cases of bluish sheen. The thing appeared to be all the colours of the rainbow but as we watched the hues lost their brilliance, faded and finally died to a neutral brown as it degenerated in the air of the tunnel.

It was the nightmare face which had wrenched such a horrifying cry from Prescott's pallid lips and it would need the genius of a Bosch or a Goya to depict such a monstrosity in pencil or paint. The features, low set on a neck which seemed to form a contiguous alignment with its chest, were insectivorous. Black tipped antennae projected from a high domed forehead; a series of mucous-plugged holes underneath seemed to serve it for breathing purposes and a tangle of tubes writhed from where the ears would have been in a human visage. A horny slot in the hinged lower jaw served it as mouth but it was the eyes which were the most unnerving and terrifying aspect of the creature. As large as soup plates and all the colours of the rainbow they seemed yet to have life of their own; all the evil of cosmic space and the wisdom of ten million years seemed to gaze from them as the creature weltered in its own juices on the floor. It resembled nothing so much as a gigantic grasshopper imbued with extra-terrestrial intelligence and I breathed a little faster as I imagined its living counterpart countless thousands of years ago.

Scarsdale, as always, was the first to recover. He stepped forward again, removing the handkerchief he had held to his nostrils, the light of enthusiasm gleaming in his eyes.

"Did you ever see the like?" he said to his companion.

"Sacred objects? Or the slaves or pets of the gigantic beings who built these tunnels?"

"Revolting but undoubtedly fascinating," said Prescott drily, though I caught in his voice the same excitement which was animating the Professor's conversation.

"Do you observe, Professor, the resemblance to the sacred baboon galleries in the tombs of the Ancient Egyptians?"

"Exactly," said Scarsdale with a chuckle. "I am glad the allusion had not escaped you. It would seem, however, that unlike the mummified remains of the Egyptians these creatures are highly perishable."

He scrabbled with the toe of one thick riding boot on the suppurating mass before him; within fifteen minutes the grasshopper-thing had dissolved, melted and evaporated, leaving nothing on the floor but a few drying membranes and some thicker muscular portions of the creature's torso.

I apologised to the Professor for not having taken any photographs.

"Oh that's all right, Plowright," he said casually. "We'll open another one straight away and you can get your photographs. Then we'll have to get back."

He took the radio microphone from me and commenced to dictate a stream of detail to Van Damm back at the base, who seemed, from his comments, as excited as our leader.

"This would happen when I remain behind," he said irritably.

"Don't worry, Van Damm," Scarsdale told him. "There's

enough material here for a hundred field workers. We will be returning within the next half an hour."

He signed off and then he and Prescott turned over another of the jars. They merely broke this with their hammers and though I was expecting it this time, the sight of those hideous eyes staring up at me made it difficult for my trembling hands to focus the camera. However, I captured a dozen or so excellent shots of the thing before it too dissolved as the other before it. I was reminded irresistibly of Poe's description of M. Valdemar disintegrating into "loathsome putrescence".

All of us, it appeared to me, were walking rapidly when we turned our backs on the gallery for our long trek back to Camp Three.

Thirteen

I

We spent two days on what Scarsdale and Van Damm had christened the embalming gallery. Once the excitement of our discovery had died away we were all kept busy on our various tasks; much to my own personal distaste Van Damm and Scarsdale had insisted on opening more of the sealed jars with their loathsome contents, though I suppose, to the scientific mind their enthusiasm was understandable. The feelings of the remainder of the expedition were more mundane and muted and it was with some reluctance that I was persuaded into photographing more of the abominations from the jars which, like their predecessors, rapidly evaporated into vapoured and gelid putrescence.

Of the beings who had embalmed the grasshopper-creatures we had no scrap of knowledge, for we found nothing within the gallery that would give us an indication; there was no embalming-room, no tools or trepanning equipment, not even a fragment of an inscription. Yet I realised Scarsdale and possibly Van Damm knew a great deal more about this strange race of ancient beings, engineers and fantastic builders who had wrought these mighty underground workings thousands of years before.

We had not yet advanced beyond the embalming gallery; this was no less than 1,000 metres long and at a conservative estimate there must have been over 10,000 of the strange jars within the building. Van Damm and Scarsdale had opened at least a dozen of the containers and every evening conversation continued long and late as the scientists debated the possibilities. The gallery ended with a similar portico to that by which we had entered. Beyond it was another massive flight of stone steps descending to a lower level; the mist hung thickly here and the steps descended into it until they were lost to sight. Strangely enough the wind still blew strongly from the north but though the vapour billowed and eddied, it still re-formed, making an impenetrable cloud, continually in motion.

Holden carried out a chemical test on the steps, the northernmost point of our penetration, and said the result showed a strong concentration of sulphur but nothing poisonous. We pitched our tents at Camp Four, near the plinth with the weird hieroglyphs and were glad of the shelter because of the grit which flew about that dusty plain. It was odd to realise that it was the same grit which was flung here and there across the surface; it had nowhere to go except within the area of that vast cavern – which, however we had no way of measuring – and so the same tiny chippings must circle and re-circle wearily over the years.

We were unable to penetrate the floor of the cavern because of the hardness of the rock so the tentpoles were secured by running them through specially designed steel centre-pieces, which Scarsdale had made in the Surrey workshops. The ropes were secured by the heavier pieces of equipment. Specially annoying to those of the milder-mannered members of the party, were the heavy machine-gun, the elephant guns and other solid pieces of ordnance which Scarsdale insisted on bringing along. These were loaded on to a small rubber-tyred trolley, like a perambulator which one or other of us had to wheel behind him wherever he went.

We were dreading mounting the great steps with this load but Scarsdale said it had to be done and no doubt it would be achieved; what our leader set out to do had a way of being accomplished.

33

I must say I was glad he was in charge and not another of Van Damm's nature. A fine scientist but too finely-wrought and argumentative and not a born leader of men like Scarsdale. The Professor had good humour and great mental toughness, which was essential for such an enterprise as that upon which we were engaged.

Holden and Prescott had been working on their own lines of research and Van Damm and the Professor were filling notebooks with their own figures and data about the insect-creatures. As my main function was photographic-historian and my dark-room and other equipment far away with the tractors, I had little practical to do in my own field, apart from maintaining my cameras and taking pictures, so that I often found myself equipment-bearer or note-taker for one of my colleagues.

This was a pleasant task, to tell the truth, for I found our surroundings oppressive in the extreme, though I did not voice my misgivings aloud. Morale can suffer in a small party in this way and I was experienced enough not to let my companions know my true feelings; Holden had already suffered a considerable shock and I knew his nerves were still ragged. The following afternoon we were all in the embalming gallery when Prescott accidentally dropped a hammer; the sound startled me, as the metallic crash went echoing strangely down the vast gallery but the effect on Holden was incredible.

He winced away, his hands over his ears and positively cowered against the tunnel wall. I went over to him and gently took him by the shoulder; he turned to me a face from which all colour had been drained. I did not like it and one had to face the unpleasant possibility that worse may be before us. The Professor was determined to press on to whatever destination these endless and devilish tunnels eventually led.

We could only follow and hope for the best. I must be fair and say that Scarsdale, Van Damm and even Prescott were made of sterner stuff. They alone continued with unabated enthusiasm though, as I have already indicated, there were sometimes occasions when even their zest for this adventure became temporarily eclipsed. On the third day, when the notebooks were filled and

masses of data had been accumulated, Scarsdale gave the order to
break camp. We left at Camp Four only a box of heavy stores the
Professor had marked as being redundant and a small pennant on
a metal rod, the symbol of the expedition.

We put all the heavier materials, including the machine-gun
into the trolley; Prescott and I were to haul this for the morning
march and neither of us were exactly impatient to tackle the long
and steep steps leading to the embalming gallery. However, it was
easier than we had anticipated, being largely a question of knack
and before the morning was over Prescott and I were becoming
quite adept at lifting the trolley over each tread of the giant steps.
The packs on our backs counterbalanced to a certain extent and
while the others strolled in front – a precise term under the circumstances – we heaved and pushed along behind, knowing that it
would be our turn to relax in the afternoon.

So we eventually descended the large flight of steps at the
other end of the gallery and were soon enveloped in the light mist
which everywhere billowed and eddied in the rising wind. It was a
heartening thing to leave the chamber of the embalmed creatures
behind us, even if we were still heading into the unknown, and
Prescott and I were several times in danger of overturning the trolley in our light-hearted descent of the steps.

Van Damm had been keeping his records still and announced,
when we were once again upon level ground, that this second set
of steps was an exact mathematical replica of the first, there being
not a quarter of an inch difference between the two. I could not
see the significance of this myself, but once again it emphasised
the fantastic precision of the unknown builders of these gloomy
edifices. There were exactly forty "treads" in each staircase, Van
Damm announced portentously. The whole of the embalming
gallery and its two sets of staircases thus occupied a length of
almost 4,000 feet, figures that must create a record in the field, Van
Damm felt.

Certainly, to Prescott and I it seemed as if we had traversed
those 4,000 feet not once but several times and Scarsdale kindly
called a halt at midday so that I and my companion could take
a much-needed break. We drank the welcome black coffee and

munched our specially produced energy biscuits gratefully, sitting
on our packs, our backs against the trolley. We were temporarily
camped about a hundred feet beyond the exit steps, seated on a
warm, dry stone floor. The light was once again brighter now that
we were out of the great stone building but the roof of the cavern,
still at some vast height above us, was obscured by the swirling
mist which, shredded this way and that by the wind, eddied and
shimmered, making everything seem as insubstantial as a dream.

Indeed, it often seemed to me, and I am sure it must have
sometimes occurred to our companions, that this was some sort
of dream, or even nightmare; an apocryphal vision in which we
moved ever onwards through the caverns of darkest night to some
awful subterranean destination at an awesome depth beneath the
surface of the wholesome earth.

The wind, still warm, blew fitfully from the north but now there
seemed the faintest echoing moan from it, which whispered sug-
gestively along the hard walls of the corridors and across the plain
towards us. The mist billowed, made strange patterns in the disturbed air and changed shape in a bewildering kaleidoscope, and
had it not been for the compasses carried by the party we should
undoubtedly have rapidly become lost.

2

During the afternoon we walked onwards by compass bearing about a mile due north, up and down an undulating surface,
almost gulley-like in its contours but not at all difficult to the party,
though the trolley occasionally proved a little troublesome when
the wheels locked while negotiating a twisting slope. The mist continued so that we did not see much of our surroundings, but the
terrain was in such marked contrast to that which we had already
traversed that it appeared as remarkable to us as the change to
Everest explorers who emerge from the tropical vegetation of the
foothills eventually to tread the eternal snows.

Visibility was about thirty feet under these conditions and at the
two o'clock break, when we consumed quite a substantial meal
cooked chemically on one of the stoves, Scarsdale prevailed upon

me to take a few photographs, recording some of the more striking rock contours. In the afternoon we walked on for another mile
or two, necessarily groping our way, with Van Damm taking frequent compass bearings. Once we seemed to hear water from far
off but we were unable to locate the source of the sound, which
appeared to shift position, no doubt due to the enveloping fog.
Van Damm and Scarsdale were scribbling busily in their notebooks
and once or twice Prescott who, like me was relieved of his trolley
duties, broke the monotony by chipping at the rocks with his little
geologist's hammer but I cannot recall ever seeing him break any
particles off, the formations were so hard.

This was possibly the most striking thing about the Great
Northern Expedition, always excepting the two great basic abso-
lutes of this enterprise and which we always came back to in our
minds at the end of each protracted and tiring day; that the whole
thing was taking place miles below the surface of the earth and
approaching a hundred miles inwards; and that the scale of the
great artefacts, such as the porticoed entrances; the tunnels; and
the embalming gallery were on a scale stupefying in comparison
with most man-made things on the earth above.

I doubted whether such works, through rock of a hardness none
of us had ever before met, could have been achieved by modern
engineers using the very latest earth-boring machinery then available. When one cast one's mind back only three thousand years, a
comparatively modest span compared with the age of the earth,
the degree of sophistication involved was almost frightening.
This was not a case where the employment of mass labour would
suffice; what we were then talking about was technology – the
machinery – for surely no works such as that could be wrought by
hand – and the knowledge to first create and then use it.

My head was full of such thoughts as we walked on, through
the endless gloom, endlessly dim light, endless mist and the endless breath of the wind on our cheeks. Occasionally my feet would
stumble or I would be brought to myself by a sudden sharp remark
by Scarsdale or Van Damm and find myself on the brink of diverg-
ing from my companion's path and about to be lost in the mist. My
mind was close to terror on such occasions and my one great fear,

that amounted to a morbid crisis, was to find myself alone in these spaces of underground nightmare. Yet such was the monotony of the place and of our walk that despite my fears, and the physical discomfort of the pack straps biting into my shoulders, I would time and again find my mind wandering into strange by-paths and fantasies.

I was ashamed when I caught myself in such digressions or when called to task by a companion as I had noted the seemingly eternal vigilance of the Professor; who always, whether he happened to be assisting with the trolley, which Van Damm and Holden were pushing this afternoon, or checking the compass, had a free hand for his naked revolver which he carried with a lanyard looped round his wrist at all times.

The throbbing noise which we had heard earlier and which had apparently ceased, now began again; but only in snatches, due to a change in the wind? But that could not be so as a compass check by Van Damm revealed that, as always, what wind there was blew lightly but fairly steadily from the north. The sound was like the faintest heartbeat, apparently from many miles away, but accompanied by emanations or vibrations which appeared to pulsate the very rock across which we walked. The party stopped for nearly an hour at one point while Scarsdale and Van Damm made certain instrument tests, but nothing specific could be ascertained from these.

Soon after we commenced walking once more the mist began to thin and we began a fairly steep climb uphill. This was so unusual that the exact time, together with latitude and longitude was noted by Scarsdale and Van Damm and more instrument bearings were taken. So far as we could see the slope up which we walked was man-made and this was exciting in itself; traces of the extremely hard and sophisticated tools which had sliced the roadway from the steel-hard rock were noted by my companions with wondering exclamations.

Van Damm and Holden were still hauling the trolley, this time with the aid of the special harness straps Scarsdale had developed, but the slope was not of sustained steepness, levelling off to a more tolerable angle shortly afterwards, so that both men declined

the help of Prescott and myself. At one stage I found myself leading the party, though Scarsdale was not far behind, swinging his
revolver in his usual vigilant fashion. Before me in the dim light
began to range a series of oblong boxes and my excited remarks
soon brought the rest of the party up.

We now advanced along a broad highway, past a slabbed obelisk bearing more of the strange inscriptions which we had already
observed. Scarsdale quickened his steps, barely pausing to note the
inscriptions, in itself a matter of wonder as he and Van Damm had
taken up many hours in the past few days in such examinations.
The trolley party was hard put to it to keep up as we three unen-
cumbered members pushed on rapidly as the strange rectangles
and cubes grew before us in the twilight.

What we were entering was a town or city of vast and unknown
size, many miles beneath the surface of the earth and whose use
and purposes were obscure to us. As we advanced farther along
the broad highway the blocks began to tower before us until I
realised that the scale upon which the town was built was as vast
as anything we had yet encountered. The blocks were windowless
and without any break in their smooth grey outlines except for
the vast portals of dressed stone, similar to those we had already
noted.

Some had smoothly traced lintels upon which were graven
strange and baffling hieroglyphs, whose very outlines looked
obscene and depraved; the highway along which we walked presently gave upon a vast square, around which the gigantic buildings
were grouped in no identifiable order or in no observable pattern.
The whole rhythmic structure of the city was complex and puz-
zling to a stranger and I had trouble with the angles and vistas,
some of which, as we passed what would be called alleys and road
junctions on the earth above, caused serious optical illusions for
the members of our party.

The square, hewn of what appeared to be enormous blocks of
stone, also seemed to run away at disturbing angles, with none
of the blocks ever quite seeming to join at the proper juncture;
instead of the paving thus formed being square or triangular it
seemed to obey no observable law or mathematical formulae so

that the eye was always being shocked by strange breaks in the formation or ugly or jarring groupings of lines. This was one of the most difficult aspects of the place and one which we were never able to overcome.

For as one advanced towards a given spot the natural law seemed to be restored; all angles met in the correct fashion, square joined to square and curve to curve. But once we had turned about or walked away from a measured point the optical illusions began again so that one began to fear for one's sanity. It was a fascinating and troubling place and one to provide endless discussion between our scientific members. Neither was my photographic work able to resolve the problem for all the studies which survived the expedition yielded nothing but the normal, however long one stared at enlargements of the prints.

We put down our equipment in the middle of the gigantic plaza and rested, sitting on an elaborately sculpted piece of stone; made from one solid slab of black material, it was elaborately incised not only with hieroglyphs but with intricately chased surfaces which broke up its outline and presented a baffling, many-surfaced structure to the viewer. Nowhere on the floor of the plaza could we detect any scratches or markings which might have been caused by the passage of vehicles in the long-distant past.

The Professor was once more consulting his typed notes and his much-thumbed transcription of The Ethics of Ygor.

"As you have no doubt observed, Van Damm," he said with a faint smile of triumph, "we are now within the ancient city of Croth."

3

"Indeed, Professor," observed Van Damm with a thin smile in return. "Here is your vindication."

And he indicated the broad spread of the city with an expressive gesture of his lean arm.

We were not long idle. Scarsdale rapidly designated the area as Camp Five and, as always on the Great Northern Expedition, we first set to erecting the tents, sorting stores, testing equipment and preparing our late afternoon meal.

Only then, when we had mounted the first sentry and set up the ugly snout of the inevitable machine-gun commanding the broad spaces of the square, did Scarsdale feel that we were at liberty to explore.

He chose for this first excursion the most massive and curious of the buildings surrounding the square; here again, there were difficulties in gaining the entrance. There was a long series of elaborately engineered ramps and ledges which we had first to surmount and then a short but exhausting flight of steps into the interior. We gained a sort of terrace at the top and turned to look back at Camp Five; the distortion of perspective there, some ten metres above the level of the square, was startling and our tents and stores appeared suspended on a heap of tumbled paving blocks.

Prescott had been left behind and on some members of our party waving, he saluted in reply; it was extraordinary to see what a fragmentary gesture it appeared, with his arm appearing completely disconnected from his body. I had some fears under the circumstances whether our weapons would be of any use under these weird optical conditions, even if we did meet a prospective target, and I voiced them on this occasion to Scarsdale. He said nothing but his eyes looked troubled.

We paused awhile on this balcony, taking in the bizarre and jumbled vista of Croth, its buildings seemingly all awry; from this height the distant throbbing which had long accompanied us was naturally more marked but I could not myself assign any specific direction to it. I had noted however, that the great broad central highway which had led us into the plaza continued out of it at the far side and that it pointed almost directly north. Along this the eternal warm wind blew steadily into our faces.

The outlines of the city seemed to fade into the amber-tinted dusk, now that the mist had disappeared, but none of us could make out any specific horizon or even a limit to the boundaries of Croth and my later photographs were to throw no further light upon this enigma. From first to last the exact geographical bounds of the city were to remain a mystery to us. While I photographed and the others noted, Scarsdale had been busy deciphering the inscription on the great portico of dressed stone towering high above our heads. He announced with surprise that the building appeared to be that of the city library and proposed to investigate further.

The interior of the building was free from dust of any sort and the light filtered down from the roof in the same manner in which the embalming gallery had been illuminated. The library initially was a disappointing experience from my point of view though to my companions the evening was one of the most exciting since we had entered this fantastic underground world. If I had expected papyrus, manuscript or great sheets of vellum, I was sadly disappointed. The place, after we had ascended an interminable series of ramps, appeared to be a series of gigantic chambers, each bearing different inscriptions along the walls.

There were hundreds of great stone benches in each chamber, ranged before a large stone edifice like a lectern; set in front of the lectern parapet was a curious metallic surface, rather like a formal representation of an eye, with incised symbols in its raised contours. It appeared to be hollow and when Scarsdale's lantern flickered into its interior the pale light disclosed what looked like a primitive mechanism of metal. Facing the lectern but hundreds of metres away was a vast pale curved stone surface which projected from the wall. To my mind it resembled nothing more than a prehistoric version of a modern lecture hall in one of our universities but Scarsdale solved the enigma in an accidental and somewhat bizarre fashion.

He disappeared from our sight for a few moments round the plinth of the lectern-structure and the next moment we were all blinded as light poured into the building; I am afraid that I cowered down behind one of the stone benches in rather an undignified manner while my companions were almost as much affected. In brilliantly delineated fashion and about a hundred feet high, vast symbols in the strange language burned at us on the far wall of the library. Then the room became dim again and Scarsdale's chuckle of satisfaction changed into a laugh of triumph.

"There is your library, gentlemen," he beamed. "This place is nothing more than a modern cinema-theatre. The information was stored something in the manner of a slide and projected on to the stone screen. What price the Lumière Brothers now?" There was a moment's stupefied silence and then the air was filled with amazed questions. Van Damm went round behind the lectern with the Professor, who explained that he had accidentally projected the rays of his helmet lantern down into the strange machine.

"My light source was far too strong, of course," he explained. "These people would have had something far subtler and less powerful, as befits the general lighting level in the ancient city of Croth. But this was undoubtedly the basis of it. There was a slide, so to speak, left in the machine. What we now have to find is the source of their power and the place where they stored their slides and we shall begin to disentangle something of the enigma of the city."

Fourteen

I

The remainder of that day was spent in a fevered chaos by Scarsdale and Van Damm in particular. Though the discovery of the picture-machine in the ancient city beneath the ground was of stupefying importance from an archaeological and historical point of view it did not excite me as much as might have been supposed. Naively, I had imagined that we were to see something like early newsreel films of this long-forgotten civilisation. Instead, the reality, when it came was much more prosaic though the Professor and his scientific companions passed an evening much like that of Lord Carnarvon and Howard Carter when they discovered the tomb of Tutankhamen.

In point of fact what the Great Northern Expedition had unearthed was equally as important, possibly more so, as the city of Croth had never even been suspected until Scarsdale and one or two obscure scholars had begun their researches into certain forbidden books. What Scarsdale and Van Damm had reanimated in what they came to call the Central Library of the city was, in fact, a visual method of projecting book pages so that hundreds of people could take part in readings at one time. This would not only have served the same function as our modern cinema for this ancient people but obviously took the place of printing for them, as by this method they had only to "publish" one particular book for the entire population.

When Van Damm himself discovered the central deposits, the raison d'être for the whole building, there was a high pitch of excitement so that I felt constrained to go back across the square to relieve Prescott, so that he could join in an occasion of outstanding interest. What the doctor and Scarsdale were so enthused about was, I had to admit to myself, something pretty spectacular in the way of breaking new ground and the Great Northern Expedition would go down in history for this alone.

What had happened was that Van Damm had accidentally dislodged a bronze knob somewhere behind the lectern; the others had felt a draught shortly after and had then noticed that a dark slot had appeared in the rear wall of the building. The lever apparently operated an ingenious series of counter-balances, sliding back a stone door cut from one slab of material but so thinly and accurately that my colleagues found it could be pushed to and fro with one hand.

What they found within, ranged upon minutely indexed stone shelves and in elaborately inscribed storage bins, were thousands of exquisitely engraved metal cylinders. How these had been created, it was not clear, as there were no tools discernible, but no doubt, Scarsdale surmised, we would find metalworkers' shops and those of other skilled artisans within the city itself.

The cylinders contained many different "frames" of material, each evidently representing a numbered page of a book or communication. The figures and symbols were punched with such delicacy and precision – letters like O having the central portion linked to the main symbol with exquisitely fine tracery work – that they could be projected complete to give a representation of the page upon the stone screen in the auditorium below.

When the cylinders were placed on a central pin on the

machine, which presumably had some sort of light source within its hollowed-out interior, it could then be revolved to bring the various faces of the work projected to the viewer's notice in proper numbered sequence. Van Damm himself had expected there to be a series of lenses, as in a modern movie projector, but this proved not to be the case.

The light, whose source remained a mystery, passed through a sort of pinhole as in that old form of camera, and by a racking device which animated the spindle, could be focused by natural light intensity, funnelling it through the metal ring on the exterior of the pulpit. We then realised that the design of the mechanism, which could only "focus" within very narrow limits, made it necessary for the whole building to be constructed to suit the apparatus. In other words, the length of the projector's "throw" determined the point at which the rear wall screen would be built. The effect can be realised by noting the projection of a sign on a glass door when sunlight repeats the pattern on a light wall some distance away.

There was no denying the tremendous nature of this discovery, and Scarsdale and those who followed would be able to learn much of this ancient civilisation from the deciphering of the cylinders. But further examination would have to wait as we had the whole city before us, wide open for exploration. I took the first watch as sentry that night and I noted that the sleep of my companions was markedly broken by the excitement of this extraordinary day.

2

The following morning Holden was left in charge of Camp Five, the inevitable machine-gun pointing its snout along the plaza in the northward direction to which we were committed. Scarsdale had decreed that for the moment we would explore only those buildings of greatest importance which lay directly on our route. It was his aim, he said, to penetrate as far to the north as possible – I myself believed he intended to seek out the source of the strange distant throbbing – and only to explore the city in depth upon our homeward journey.

It was about ten a.m. when the party left, Scarsdale and Van Damm leading, as always, and myself, as the least scientifically useful member of the Expedition in the rear. The expendable position Prescott called it jocularly, and though we all laughed, it was a somewhat macabre joke to my mind. But perhaps Prescott was a more effective psychologist than he realised as his words served to sharpen my wits so that I kept a more than usually alert watch from my vulnerable rearward position.

The northward-leading thoroughfare, which nevertheless had a disturbing optically-distorted quality about it, led away through what in a normal city would be described as the suburbs. The size of the buildings diminished as we left the square, though they were still upon an impressive scale. The light, to which we had now become accustomed, was of the same overall strength so that we did not need any artificial aids to illuminate our way. The distant throbbing was growing more distinct as we tramped onwards for more than an hour; the structures here, into which we occasionally ventured, were nothing more than empty square boxes with no windows but merely steps upwards, a portico and a square door punched in the surface.

The material was the same steel-hard stone that we had already observed. Before we left the square proper we also ventured into one or two other large buildings but despite the inscriptions on the lintels we could not make out their purpose; one appeared to be a sort of office, with large square flat slabs of stone which might have served as counters. There were no chairs or furniture of any other kind. The floors were of the same smooth, interlocking stones which gave the aberrant optical effects I had already noted and were free of dust or detritus of any kind.

The second building seemed to be some sort of warehouse, full of jars and square vessels, all sealed and there were also piles of thin stone slabs which bore incised writing in a language different to the hieroglyphs, Scarsdale said. We did not open any of the sealed jars or boxes, in view of our previous experiences in the embalming gallery. The roadway led slightly uphill, always due north, and with other roads, built on a smaller scale running at exact mathematical radii from it; almost always at right-angles. Just before noon we came to a sensational innovation, a strange, four-arched bridge, that seemed to be suspended from either side of a large stream about forty feet wide, but of some unknown engineering principle as the bottoms of the arches nowhere appeared to touch the water.

This caused a great deal of excited speculation between Scarsdale, Van Damm and Prescott and it was quite some while before any of us ventured on it, as it seemed so frail. It proved to be of some unfamiliar metal and even more bizarre, nowhere was there any evidence of nuts, bolts, rivets or welding as known in the modern world.

Scarsdale summed it up well when he turned to me and said, "If I didn't know the thing was impossible I would say that this whole structure was carved from one block of metal by some gigantic force."

Van Damm's face was white as he gazed around him in the gloom.

"Just why do you say it is impossible, Professor?" he said quietly. "I should say this is one word which it would be unwise to use down here, judging by what we've already seen."

It was the only time I had seen Scarsdale at a loss for words. He coughed awkwardly and shifted his huge feet in the riding boots.

"Perhaps you're right, Van Damm," he said mildly. "One cannot always judge properly without all the relevant data. I should perhaps have qualified my remarks."

Van Damm said nothing in reply but went to the smoothly burnished balcony of the bridge, which ran in a shining, slightly curved arc to the farther shore. He gazed down into the turgid, rippling water, which gave off a slight luminescence. There was a current here and it ran back in the direction from which we had come. I ventured to say that this river probably drained into the lake which we had crossed and was gratified to learn that the leaders of the party were already of the same opinion.

Nothing showed on the surface of the river; there appeared to be no life in the depths; and no flotsam or any other debris was carried down. At least, not while we were there and we lingered for an hour in that strange spot.

At last we moved on, reaching the far shore without incident. I looked back towards the city but it was already lost in the haze. I could not help reflecting, with a sinking of the heart, that we were committing ourselves more and more into the interior of this bizarre and terrible place, with every day that passed; if anything malignant were encountered it would be very difficult, if not impossible to fight the long miles back.

We lunched on the opposite bank of the stream, where there were no buildings or vegetation of any kind, just the bare unyielding rock and sandy particles of grit to which we had long become used. Scarsdale had decided by this time that we would continue in the northwards direction together and to do this it was necessary that Holden rejoin us. I contacted him by radio – we had been in touch at intervals all the morning – and Van Damm said that he would go back. The two men would then load the machine-gun and heavy equipment on the trolley and rejoin us in the afternoon.

Van Damm had been gone several minutes and had in fact disappeared in the haze across the bridge only a short while before when there came a sudden stammer from the machine-gun which reverberated and echoed in the most awful way across the miles of caverns. There were separate and distinct bursts but the muted thunder of the explosions was constantly repeated under the cave roof and created such a menacing effect that our party instinctively cowered away as though we ourselves were under fire.

The noise was so unexpected and so shocking that none of us could at first think what it meant; that Holden had fired at something was obvious but this underground atmosphere was so arid and lifeless that it was difficult to think of a possible target.

I found Prescott at my side; his suggestion was that of a signal but Scarsdale immediately ruled that out as Holden had only to use his radio. We expected Van Damm would immediately hurry on to Holden's assistance and indeed he came through on his handset almost at once. I then tried to reach Holden on the radio link but with no success.

"Keep trying," Scarsdale told me, almost savagely. His bearded face looked more like a Viking than ever as he gazed about him, his revolver cocked and ready for use. I remembered then the fate of the dwarf Zalor and realised what had never been absent from our leader's mind; that this underground world harboured many ancient and evil things which would only reveal themselves when they were ready.

"Has Holden been attacked, do you think?" Prescott asked the Professor.

Scarsdale shook his head impatiently. "We shall know in good time," he said crisply. "I blame myself for splitting the party. Holden was possibly the wrong person to leave on his own like this. His nerves have been uneven ever since we found the dwarf's body."

I looked at him in surprise as it was the first time he had ever directly mentioned the incident.

I shall never forget the long hour we sat by the bridge parapet, looking across the stygian water and listening to the incessant crackle of the radio set; my own nerves were stretched high and I expected minute by minute to hear another shattering series of explosions from the machine-gun. But nothing came and my tension eventually died away.

Then, at about two o'clock in the afternoon to our intense relief we heard Holden's voice on the radio. He apologised for what he knew must have been a startling incident. He had fired, he said, at something which was moving towards him between the buildings at the edge of the plaza. He had then gone off to investigate, leaving the radio, and had only just returned.

Scarsdale moved to take the microphone from me at this point. I forget his exact words but his clipped tones and reproving, if urbane, remarks had the desired effect; Holden did not afterwards forget the Professor's strict instructions.

"Well," he said at length. "There appears to be no harm done and I think you can take it that anything down here would be alien to human life as we know it. We will not come back but I'll await your report when you return with the doctor."

Scarsdale instructed Holden to dismantle the equipment; he and Van Damm could then investigate the area further on their way to re-join us. He would keep the radio link open constantly from now on. A few minutes later Van Damm's tetchy voice came through. When the two men came across the bridge pushing the trolley full of heavy equipment later in the afternoon, Holden told his story in person to Scarsdale as we all crowded round. He had been sitting in the square making notes, he said, when he became aware of some faint shadowy thing which appeared to flit between the far buildings at the end of the plaza.

The occurrence was so unusual that he kept watch on the one point for several minutes; he had thought that it was the optical illusion which we had found common to the city but he soon realised that a large "hopping thing" as he described it, was moving about between the block-like structures at the edge of the square and gradually coming closer. Not surprisingly, he did not like this, and rapidly got behind the machine-gun.

After another quarter of an hour passed, the thing, which appeared to be grey in hue and of enormous size, stood still; Holden got the uncomfortable impression that he himself was being studied and he reached for his binoculars. He had difficulty in focusing the glasses but as soon as the thing began to come into reasonably clear view, its aspect was so disturbing that Holden became greatly agitated and was unable to hold the binoculars properly. It was only a few seconds after that before he let off a burst with the machine-gun, followed by two others, as the thing made off into the distance.

Courageously, under the circumstances, but foolishly as it now appeared, Holden then set off with one of the elephant rifles to see whether he had wounded the creature. The satisfying noise of the machine-gun had given him back his courage and he hoped to find whether he had hit it. He did find one or two of the flattened bullets from the gun lying at the edge of the square but so far as he could see, there was no sign of the creature and of course the buildings themselves were of too hard a material for the impact of the bullets to make any impression on them.

It was only after he had reported to us on the radio and Van Damm had reached him that they had seen any other evidence of the creature. He and Van Damm had taken a slightly different route out of the city, in order to pass by the spot where the hopping thing had been seen.

"There was a trail of slime leading off the edge of the square," said Van Damm grimly. "The stench was awful and we didn't follow it up."

Fifteen

I

We didn't talk much about this among ourselves. As if by tacit consent each member of the Great Northern Expedition busied himself with the work in hand. Scarsdale wanted to press on to the limit of exploration in the northern direction; that was his prime purpose in mounting the project at all, he emphasised. We would be able to take in the ancient city of Croth on the return journey; he planned to spend a month charting, photographing and investigating every last building and artefact, he assured us.

There would also be a system of "leave", with two members at a time returning to the outside air for a fortnight, both for relaxation and to safeguard the lines of communication. This seemed an excellent idea to me as I for one found the life underground oppressive and chilling, with the never-changing light and the haunting silence, broken only by the faint thumping of the great pulse in the distance.

Scarsdale also made the implicit promise in his remarks that we would deal with the strange creature seen by Holden on our return; that there might be more of them and that somehow they might prevent our return to the outside world did not seem to have occurred to him. Or rather, to correct myself, I was sure that it had, but that he did not want to go into any detailed explanation for reasons of his own. I remembered then that the Great Northern Expedition was to crown Scarsdale's work of a lifetime and that he would naturally oppose anything which stood between him and its completion. He was determined to reach the farthermost northern limits where beat the strange heart we had travelled toward so long and to this end he was prepared to overlook any dangers and difficulties which might loom large in the mind of a lesser man.

Against this I had to weigh the possible dangers to the other, less knowing members of the party and whether Scarsdale, as leader, was entitled to risk the lives of his companions in this way; I maintained in the end that he was. After all, he had made the same proposition to each one of us in the great study back in Surrey, and had emphasised the dangers. After weighing things up each had made the identical decision; which implied absolute trust in Scarsdale as head of the party; in his integrity; and in his judgement as a leader of men.

I had also to remember his great hardships and bitter disappointments in penetrating so far on his previous journey and then being forced to return – at great risk to his own life. I put all these questions, arguments and counter-arguments to myself as we walked onwards through the twilight for the rest of that day and I came ever to the same conclusion. That we had trusted Scarsdale this far – in my own case quite blindly – and we were, on balance, correct to continue to trust him right up to the edge of what many people would call, under those circumstances, folly.

Having come to this conclusion I marched with an easier mind; we saw nothing and heard nothing on this stretch, save that the wind now blew stronger, freshening to a fairly stiff breeze at times and that the slow rhythmic thump, like a pile-driver, was more audible and quite distinct. Van Damm and I were manoeuvring the trolley over fairly easy ground; there was a very slight gradient, leading uphill which was not, however, at all fatiguing. I did most of the pushing while Van Damm walked at the front, occasionally steadying the equipment with his hand.

Scarsdale was leading, naked revolver drawn, while Prescott brought up the rear, also with a cocked and loaded weapon at the ready. Both Scarsdale and Prescott had the lamps in their helmets switched on, in case of emergency, and in order to augment the existing light which still shone duskily from some unimaginable roof far above our heads. But the terrain was gradually changing; from a level plain such as that which we had crossed to reach the embalming gallery, the sides were gradually closing in to form a large tunnel about forty feet across. Here Scarsdale decided to halt for the night so that in case of any alarm we should have plenty of open space across which any intruder would have to advance.

We passed an undisturbed night, each of us taking two-hour turns at sentry; this time we did not pitch the tents but simply slept in the open. Van Damm had found an oil lamp from somewhere and by its reassuring pool of golden light he sat long into the night hours – we still measured time by earth's days and nights – and made his endless algebraic calculations in his series of notebooks. One of the most astonishing things about this expedition to my mind was the fact that the leaders obviously knew so much more about its purpose than the rank-and-file.

Yet we three were quite content to follow, each using his own specialised skills, none of us really knowing anything of the big questions that were taxing the complex minds of Scarsdale and Van Damm. I knew that they would, of course, tell us everything when they were ready but it argued a high degree of trust on the part of such highly qualified specialists as Holden and Prescott. With these and other such thoughts I passed an hour after coming off the midnight duty and my last vision was of Van Damm polishing his glasses in the cheerful aura of the lamp before sleep found me.

2

We were breakfasted and packed by six the next morning and on the move shortly after. There had been nothing to report during the night from any of the sentries but despite this Scarsdale insisted that Holden and Prescott, who were wheeling the trolley on this occasion, should mount the machine-gun on its tripod, ready for instant use. He also ordered that each of us should carry a Very pistol in addition to side arms. This was not only for signalling purposes – after all we had the radio link for that – but to illuminate anything which we wanted to investigate. We had already tried firing the pistols some days earlier to see if they would reveal the height and extent of the roofs of the gigantic cave system. While spectacularly illuminating the cloudy distances, they had been remarkably unsuccessful for that purpose.

Fired at the "sky" they curved upwards for hundreds of feet and on exploding burned as a faint glow beneath the layers of misty vapour which hid the roof from us and which gave the illusion of the sky. But as they came closer to the ground they gave a brilliant and blinding light compared to the low intensity illumination we had been used to. To detect ground targets they would be incomparably useful. I for one, though secretly grumbling at the bulkiness and weight of the pistol I was forced to carry, later came to realise their usefulness in our situation and on at least one occasion the Very lights saved my life.

Soon after we started the day's march the tunnel became narrower – it was now down to about thirty feet wide and it then started splitting up into branching tunnels and diversions; when we first came upon a tributary, something most unusual in our exploration so far, Scarsdale dealt with the matter quite simply. He chose the largest tunnel which still pointed to the north and down which the warm wind blew. There was a purpose behind the master tunnel as Van Damm called it and this remained the principle of selection throughout.

Scarsdale had also organised elaborate precautions for finding our way back from the labyrinth in which we were now picking our way. In addition to simple chalked arrows on walls and the tunnel floor, which reminded me of childhood games, small metal discs were fastened by suction pads at particularly difficult and elaborate junctions. These were miniature radio beacons which Holden and Prescott had developed and the radio equipment we carried could be tuned in to them to guide us back.

"Unless anything realises their purpose and removes them while we are gone," said Van Damm grimly. I was impressed by the fact that he did not say "anyone" and it was a thought which did not bear dwelling on. I queried in my mind yet again whether in fact the strange creature Holden had spotted was responsible for the unique and horrible manner in which the dwarf Zalor had met his end. And leading on from that, whether such creatures – I could not imagine that one only would be unique in such a vast underground complex and presupposed there must be others – had something to do with the people who had carried out the ancient embalming processes on the weird insect-like beings in the jars.

We walked slightly uphill for an hour without seeing or hearing anything untoward; the pulsations were becoming much clearer now and seemed to vibrate the very ground over which we advanced. Unmistakably also, and this represented a fantastic change in our conditions, it was becoming lighter. Van Damm was the first person to notice this I believe, though typically he kept it to himself for almost half an hour until he was absolutely certain. And indeed the process was so subtle and delicate that the floor, walls and the distant vista along the corridor we were traversing etched itself fraction by fraction on our retinas, so imperceptible that it took minutes to realise that the scene around us was "developing" itself, much as a photographic plate creates an image in the photographer's dish.

I saw Holden's face change to a mask of wonder in the rapidly strengthening light; it was like being reborn after months in semi-darkness though in reality I supposed we had been underground for something like a fortnight. But here a day could seem like a month with the feeble glow of the artificial sky and the shifting patterns forming in the wispy afterglow which served for atmosphere in this place.

Scarsdale and Van Damm exchanged triumphant glances and I realised that this was what they had been expecting all along; that the central premise of the whole expedition, probably known only to them, was at last coming to life before their eyes, transformed from dusty parchment and well-thumbed typescript and page after page of abstruse calculations.

"The Trone Tables were right, Professor," Van Damm muttered, his thin savant's face alight with strange dreams. "Allow me to congratulate you, sir."

And impulsively, he moved forward, and began to pump Scarsdale's hand.

The big man blinked slowly in the strengthening paleness that glowed along the walls of the corridor, obviously moved. I stepped to one side, leaving them to their moment of quiet victory. The others sensed that something important was about to happen and as if by a common impulse withdrew to a discreet distance.

Van Damm and the Professor stood together for the next ten

minutes, consulting their notebooks and tables of crabbed notes before rejoining us.

"All will be made clear to you, gentlemen, very soon," said Scarsdale crisply. "You have all been patient and extremely forbearing, I must say. I calculate – and I am sure my colleague here will confirm – that we are nearing our objective; the end of our epic journey and one that will, I am sure, be destined to go down in the epoch-making explorations of this first half of the twentieth century. I say this without self-importance or undue pomposity and without taking the credit to myself. I could have done nothing without the unstinted efforts of each of you and I would like to thank you here and now for everything that you have done and will do before we bring the task to a successful conclusion."

It had been a long speech for the Professor and he had evidently been deeply moved; he paused for a moment, his face flushed and the light shining on his strong features etching his beard with shadow so that he looked more than ever like an engraving of some age-old god or perhaps a Viking raider from the North.

"An honour and a pleasure, my dear Scarsdale," said Van Damm awkwardly, on behalf of us all.

"Well then," said Scarsdale, with a return to his old manner. "We press on. But first a commonsense precaution."

He crossed over to the trolley and grunted as he rummaged about among its contents. Presently he opened a sealed package of canvas. He handed its contents round among us. I found myself clutching a pair of deeply tinted snow goggles with heavy elasticised straps.

"A curious item, perhaps," said the Professor. "You possibly wondered why these were shipped. You're about to find out. I have many theories but I don't know how strong this light will get."

There was a perceptible stirring among the party at this and Prescott queried, "Do you mean to say that we are approaching the open air?"

Scarsdale shook his head.

"This light comes from a subterranean source of whose origins I am not certain. There may be some danger without the goggles. I would like everyone to put them on when I give the order. And not to remove them under pain of the most serious consequences."

This promise was rapidly given by all of us, of course, and when we had each stowed the goggles away where they could easily be reached, we resumed our march.

Holden turned to me as we walked together, pulling the trolley. I could see his face more clearly now and was shocked to note that there were dark shadows under his eyes and his lips were a startling white. He seemed but the shadow of the man who had set out with us so enthusiastically from the Professor's Surrey home; looking back on that hectic period it seemed to me now that it had taken place not only long ago but on another planet, so alien and bizarre were our present surroundings. Most of us too had lost all sense of time and we could have been many weeks here, instead of the minutely documented days that we had spent beneath the surface of the earth. Even the time since leaving Croth seemed infinitely distant.

I put my face close to Holden as he mumbled something; his ravaged features looked like a steel engraving in the slowly growing light. I had to ask him to repeat his sentence, his words were so slow and hesitant.

What I eventually made out was the broken sentence, "I cannot go on."

I looked at him sharply. I saw now that he was trembling slightly as though he were suffering from fever. There had been such a marked deterioration in him since I had last had occasion to observe him a few days earlier that I was startled. But of course the dimness of the light in which we had previously been immured would have made it difficult to observe his condition in detail. I stopped abruptly as my companion's legs gave; the trolley veered and tipped against the wall of the tunnel with a sharp grating sound. Holden's knees buckled and he tried feebly to support himself with one hesitant hand on the metal railing of the trolley, failed and slipped to the ground in an insensate heap.

My shout brought Scarsdale and the others running back towards me. I had already turned Holden over but Scarsdale elbowed me aside with a muttered apology. I busied myself in removing the trolley so that the Professor and Van Damm could examine our companion properly. There was little further I could do so I stood off at a distance with Prescott while the two scientists busied themselves over the huddled form on the tunnel floor. One foot of the recumbent man lay at a grotesque angle.

Van Damm got up presently and fumbled among the kit on the trolley.

"Is there anything I can do to help?" I asked him.

The doctor shook his head. He looked puzzled.

"He's fainted but there is more to it than that," he said. "Apart from nerves, that is."

He paused as though he had said too much.

"I know he had a bad shock when we found the dwarf's body," I said. "There's no secret about that."

My manner must have seemed a little short for the doctor shot me a sharp, shrewd glance.

"I don't mean only that, my dear Plowright," he said. "Holden was one of the fittest men along on this party. If I didn't know better I'd say he was suffering from some form of pernicious anae-mia. He's in a comatose condition. I'd say he's collapsed from sheer physical exhaustion. His nerves were strung-up, yes, but this is not the cause of his condition."

He refused to be drawn any further and went back to the two men, taking the flask of brandy with him. Prescott and I stood in the strengthening light that flooded from the long tunnel before us and waited for the verdict.

Sixteen

I

In the end it was arranged that Van Damm would stay with Holden while Prescott and I, led by the Professor, would press on towards the strengthening light which beckoned in front of us. It took some element of self-sacrifice on the part of Van Damm to suggest remaining behind and I was near to admiring him at that moment. Despite the assumed waspishness between the two of them Scarsdale and Van Damm were close, and they had together hammered out a successful formula for the Great Northern Expedition. It seemed as though Van Damm had cheated himself of the shared glory if we now discovered something even more extraordinary in the growing luminescence of that subterranean place.

Moved by these and other considerations I had myself volunteered to remain behind with Holden, who was now conscious and able to speak. But I was immediately overruled by the two heads of the expedition; apart from being deputy leader Van Damm also had specialist medical knowledge. What could I do if there were some emergency beyond my own sparse rudiments of first-aid? No, said Scarsdale, it would not do; besides, he added sotto voce to me, as we stood alone for a moment, apart from the others, he might have need of my agility and strength at the front.

Prescott was experienced in the use of firearms and would be needed also; so it was arranged. We presently set off, led by the Professor carrying a naked revolver, followed closely behind by Prescott and myself pushing the trolley. In addition to the light machine-gun, ready on its tripod, Scarsdale had also laid out a number of hand grenades within easy reach. I watched these grim preparations with growing disquiet. I did not know what the Professor expected to find but it was obviously something large and inimical to human life if we needed protection on this scale.

We had gone only a few hundred yards beyond the point where we had left our two companions before there was an appreciable strengthening of the light; not only its intensity but its quality. It had a flickering, throbbing property which was hard on the eyes; it seemed to pulsate in time with the vibrating pulse which beat ahead of us with ever-increasing strength.

We could now see our way quite clearly by this illumination; the branching tunnels still led away to left and right but there was no doubt that the one we were following was the correct one; it led, despite slight curvatures to either side, unerringly to the north and both the light and the throbbing pulse which had the strength of a muted kettledrum played at a distance, undoubtedly emanated from this source. I did, in fact, at Scarsdale's suggestion, try one of the branching tributaries to the right but the light faded in a very few seconds and the vibrating rhythm of the pulse-beat with it.

Prescott now drew to my attention some more of the curiously incised hieroglyphs which were carved at various points on the side of the tunnel we were following; I wondered perhaps whether they might be distance marks but the Professor thought not. He puzzled at them for a few minutes and then announced sharply that they were mathematical formulae whose purpose for the moment escaped him. I gave him a long searching glance and by the way he lowered his eyelids I felt that he was not speaking the truth.

The markings appeared to me to be no different to the other inscriptions in the ancient language and I could see no formulae which would make any mathematical symbols. However, I guessed that the Professor had his own reasons for not translating the signs; it may have been that they had a sinister import and that he had no wish to alarm us.

I did, however, persuade him and Prescott to pose for some pictures by one of the plaques and then changed round to allow Prescott to photograph myself with the Professor. As it turned out this was the only picture of the expedition to survive which showed myself. By now we had little or no need of any artificial illumination and could see perhaps a quarter of a mile ahead along the tunnel. It was this factor – and thank God for it – which was instrumental in saving our lives.

A sudden shout from Prescott put my nerves on edge. He was at my elbow, pointing.

"There, man, there. The slime trails!"

I saw what he meant a moment later, before the awful stench was brought to us on the warmth of the strengthening wind. Great, slug-like smears on the surface of the tunnel which led off into unknown debouchments at the side.

Scarsdale nodded as I caught him up. He had obviously already seen them.

"I understood Van Damm saw this back in the square in the city," I said. "Why is it we haven't come across them before?"

"Because they didn't want us to see them before," said the Professor grimly. "They erased the trails. Now it doesn't matter."

I had no time to digest this, fortunately, for we were now, as though by instinct, quickening our pace and hurrying on in the ever-increasing white light which continued to radiate from somewhere ahead of us. I put my handkerchief tightly over my nostrils. We crossed the slime-trails a moment later; they were awful, more than an inch thick, and our boots skidded on them. I took one look at Prescott's face and it registered the same loathing and disgust I felt on mine.

Then we were through and out on to dry tunnel floor beyond. The great central highway was now rising slightly and curving to the right; the wind blew quite strongly, though still warm, but with a raw, charnel edge to it. The pulse-beat was rising to a crescendo that echoed uncomfortably in the ears. And with it the light level was rising to a vivid intensity. Its pulsations, that echoed the heart-beats in our ears, were becoming uncomfortable to the eye and without waiting for Scarsdale's instructions we each put on our goggles, as at some central order.

At the same moment Scarsdale radioed through to Van Damm and I was reassured to hear the doctor's fluting voice in reply. He had nothing to report and Holden appeared to be gaining strength. He thought he might be fit to move within an hour or two. Scarsdale in signing off, said he would leave the radio-link open from now on. Prescott and I were finding the trolley a little heavier with the steepness of the slope and Scarsdale put his great shoulder to it, which helped considerably. So we tottered onwards up the steeply increasing gradient to where the blinding light mingled with the drum-beat of the unknown pulse.

2

My ear-drums were almost bursting and my sight glazed with the pulsating light as we gained the top of the slope. We all three let go of the trolley and staggered like drunken men to where something like a gigantic door opened and closed to the drum-beat. Even with the goggles the glare was so intense that I had to close my eyes to mere slits. I slumped to the floor of the cave and with Scarsdale and Prescott at my side forced myself to gaze at that stupefying vision.

The light was so white and incandescent it seemed to come
from some realm beyond the stars while it was so bound up with
the pulsations that it almost burst the brain. I turned to Scarsdale.
His face was like a vivid etching in the white heat which bathed all
of the scene before us. Apart from the rock floor which stretched
away from us there was nothing else visible in the world but the
palely writhing light-source which might well have led to eternity.

"The Great White Space!" said Scarsdale, his hand tightening
on my arm, his face aglow with knowledge. His thoughts were
etched as almost visible manifestations on the pale fire which
writhed on his countenance. He shouted above the roaring rumble
which mingled with the pulse-beat like a gigantic furnace.

"The Door to the Universe. The Door through which the Great
Old Ones pass and re-pass."

I did not profess to understand what he was saying and pre-
sumed merely that he was naturally overcome by the vastness
and unexpectedness of the vision. I heard Prescott cry out then
and turning, saw that his face bore an expression of loathing and
horror. Scarsdale had just commenced a transmission to Van
Damm but he stopped in mid-sentence. A loathsome putresence
had begun to manifest itself within the tunnel. It emanated out
there somewhere beyond the veil of blinding light which shone
before us like a million suns.

Then I saw what Prescott had already observed and almost
lost my sanity. How shall I explain or describe the nodding horror
which edged its way from the pale luminosity into our view? It was
a colossal height which accounted for the vast doors through which
we had ourselves passed on our way to this abode of abomination.
The thing made a squelching, slopping noise as it progressed in a
series of hopping jerks and with the noise came the stench, borne
to our nostrils by the warmly acrid wind which blew as out of the
vastnesses of primeval space.

The very brightness of the light which surrounded it with a
white-hot glow mercifully prevented too close a view. The head of
the thing, which appeared to change shape as it hopped along, was
something like a gigantic snail or slug, while vague, lobster-like
claws depended from its middle. In general form it appeared to be

monadelphous; that is, a number of filament-like particles made up what we should call a body, uniting into one bundle from which depended the claw-members.

Worse still, other similar forms appeared from behind it, like an army of half-blind beings, surging in from the glowing air like subterranean creatures from the depths of the sea. But most unnerving of all was the noise which emanated from them. From a lowing bellow like cattle at the bass end of the scale to the high shrill mewing of a cat at the other. Can anyone blame us if we all three, seized by some primeval impulse, manhandled the trolley, backed swiftly with it and – I am not ashamed to say it, even of the great Professor Clark Ashton Scarsdale – ran for our lives?

Seventeen

I

My breath hissed and wheezed in my throat as we ran blindly down the tunnel. At one point Prescott stumbled and the trolley, freed from his grasp, veered into the side wall. There was a crash and it lurched, bumped again and then turned over with a clatter. I heard a cry but I merely leap-frogged over the belt of the machine-gun, which was stuck awry on its tripod, and pounded on. A few minutes later Scarsdale, Prescott and I, shame-faced and panting leaned against the wall of the tunnel in a spot where dusk began once again to take over and assessed the position.

There were no recriminations. This was not the time and the matter was too important for such trivia. Scarsdale first contacted Van Damm and warned him of what we had seen, in more restrained terms, of course. When he had finished I had my first chance to question him.

"What you are saying, Professor," I said reluctantly, "is that those creatures are from space? That despite the fact we know ourselves to be irrefutably miles beneath the surface of the earth, there is some sort of door which leads to the planets? Is such a thing mathematically possible?"

"This is so," said Scarsdale sombrely. "It would take too long to go into the theory now. But this is what I most emphatically believe and what I expected to find. These Great Old Ones pass and re-pass from their errands beyond the stars, for what purpose and by what means we know not. Man is just at the beginning of knowledge in these things. My task in coming here was twofold; firstly, to establish contact if that were possible and to forge links of friendship. Secondly, if that were not possible to warn the world of their presence here beneath the earth."

"The Ethics of Ygor and your other documents presumably detailing these possibilities?" I said.

"Exactly," said the Professor sombrely. His breathing was more shallow now and his eyes smouldered in the dim light of the tunnel.

"The lights I spoke of presaged a new invasion of the creatures. What we must do now, apart from extricating ourselves, is to record these beings as warning to the outside world. And that means photographs."

"You surely do not intend to go back?" said Prescott in a strange voice, his jaw hanging slackly.

"We must, if we intend to survive," said the Professor crisply. "We must recover the trolley which contains all our heavy arms. If we have to fight our way out we shall never do so without their aid. You forget Zalor. They dealt with him and erased all traces of their presence to allow us to penetrate this far on our outward journey. Do not forget the side tunnels. The way back may be swarming with the creatures. And I have not yet finished studying them!"

Prescott looked at Scarsdale with something resembling awe and admiration. Already the big man was on his feet, revolver in hand.

"Only two hundred yards, gentlemen," he said encouragingly. "Not far for the sake of humanity!"

We all ran blindly back down the tunnel into the strengthening light, hoping against hope that our echoing passage would not stir up more of those monstrous shadows. Vain hope. Scarsdale and I reached the trolley first, heaved it upright. Prescott righted the machine-gun tripod. There came an angry mewing from far off down the corridor, where dim shapes glowed in that subterranean light. Prescott screamed and then the stammer of the machine-gun sounded with heart-stopping suddenness. Bullets whined and ricochetted from the walls, striking sparks in the gloom and acrid smoke enveloped the group as the Professor and I tugged the trolley rearwards before running back to take up our stand either side of our companion. I had just time to take three pictures before they were on us.

The dim air was full of great lumbering shapes. Somehow I found the butt of a Very pistol and fired; the lurid glow of the flare illuminated a scene of Gothic horror. With mewing hisses great forms from the pit undulated and advanced towards us, their claw-like tentacles reaching languidly. The machine-gun fired again and I felt my pistol hot as I instinctively squeezed the trigger until the chamber was empty.

"No good," Prescott was shouting in my ear. "The bullets appear to make no impression."

Indeed, I had myself noticed that the holes torn in the jelly-like substance of the things seemed to close up immediately, as water fills a footprint in a swamp.

Scarsdale, as always, had the better idea. He had seized the rack of grenades and lobbed them deliberately, one after the other, into the herd of lowing, milling beings. As we cowered on the ground the air vibrated to the explosions, the thumps followed by a rain of lethal fragments. Shrill mewing cries followed, cut by bright flame. We did not stop to see what damage had been done.

"Get the trolley!" Scarsdale shouted. "We must not lose the equipment."

His pistol flamed again as we fell back, the three of us blundering against one another in what amounted to near panic. I tripped and fell, felt Prescott's boots pass over my recumbent body. Somehow I slipped and slithered back along the corridor, filled now with acrid smoke and the stench of cordite fumes. Scarsdale and I heaved and pushed at the trolley, which seemed to be off balance. It came free then and we trundled it down the corridor into the rapidly dying light.

We heard Prescott scream again then. It had a note of high, squealing urgency. I turned to see that he had attempted to manhandle the machine-gun away on his own. One of the great slopping things had its tentacle around his foot; some inky fluid like a squid enveloped Prescott as I watched. His cry was abruptly cut and lost in the mewing hiss of the creature. Prescott was now high in the air as I lowered my pistol uselessly; I hesitate to use the word but it was my impression that our companion was ingested into the monadelphous shape of the viscous being which held him fast.

Both Scarsdale and I momentarily broke then and with the strength of men pushed beyond their limit hurled and shoved and wrenched the trolley down the slope and away from that hellish scene and into the welcoming blanket of the healthy and merciful semi-darkness.

2

We sat against the tunnel wall in the dim light and grimly pondered our situation; we were now over a mile from the scene of the confrontation and had somewhat recovered our senses. Following our headlong flight and when we found we were no longer pursued, Scarsdale and I had started to push the trolley like drunken men, always facing south towards the now desired darkness. The light had long ago faded to the lustreless dimness to which we had become accustomed and our eyes had now once more adjusted.

We were in a serious situation and if, as Scarsdale had already suggested, our opponents, enemies or whatever we cared to call them, had some means of cutting us off by using other tunnels we must be finished. Neither of us had any doubt that poor Prescott was dead and a like fate awaited the rest of us. Though these and other grim thoughts chased themselves through my whirling brain, strangely enough my nerves were now more under control than they had been when we knew nothing of the dangers we faced.

But it is often so and I had noted this on the expedition in the Arizona desert to which I have already referred. Over and again

Scarsdale had reproached himself for being caught in such a manner. He held himself responsible for Prescott's death, and so he was, of course; but no-one could have done anything else under the circumstances and had our late colleague not slipped there is no doubt that Scarsdale's decisive actions and heroic behaviour in the crisis would have enabled all three of us to get clear safely. I had told him as much but in the last hour he had retreated into himself and apart from occasional references to his inked notes, which he held on to through every crisis, both internal and external, he spoke but little.

This in itself worried me and I had kept the radio link with Van Damm open, more for something to do than with any real thought of maintaining our usual routine. I had, of course, given the doctor a somewhat more restrained picture of our situation; so far as Holden was concerned, he was about the same and Van Damm was, of course, keeping a very sharp look-out, after our warnings.

For some reason Scarsdale and I now found the trolley something of a burden; I myself think the axle must have become twisted when it fell against the tunnel wall or perhaps the defect had occurred during our flight. At any rate both of us now thought it a problem, even without the weight of the machine-gun, and we had considered, more than once, abandoning some of its contents.

Fortunate indeed, that we did not do so, as events were to prove. Scarsdale stirred at my side and something of the old energy now glowed from his eyes. He patted my knee clumsily as he got up.

"Sorry about my taciturnity back there, Plowright," he said. "I've a lot to think about."

"It wasn't your fault," I said for perhaps the tenth time. "We have made stupefying discoveries and these, backed with my photographs, should be sufficient . . ."

I had got up by this time but he broke into my flow of speech, with a vehement shake of his head.

"No, no," he said. "You do not understand. This whole thing, I see now, is too fantastic for belief. What real proof could we show people? You do see now why I never went into details of what I really expected to find."

We both put our shoulders to the trolley and heaved it along between us. Progress was slow, as we had also to watch our rear; my ears were now tuned to hypersensitive frequencies and I found the crackle from the radio linking us with Van Damm a definite intrusion.

I replied to Scarsdale with some commonplace. How could I really reply to him? He was right, of course; what could we say? How could we warn the outside world of our discoveries? And even so, half of Scarsdale's suppositions remained unproved. Mathematicians could no doubt find a method of equating the interior of the earth with the exterior vastnesses of space but I could imagine the response from the average scientific mind, deeply entrenched in library or laboratory in half a dozen European countries. Not that I blamed them. I myself would be in the van of the sceptics were I in their place.

Perhaps the sceptics could be right and we ourselves the victims of some strange dimensional illusion? Self-hypnotism? God knows these dark caves were enough to make anyone's sanity totter. Or perhaps the Great White Space, as Scarsdale called it, was real enough but merely a three-dimensional cavity within the earth but possessed of such blinding luminosity that it seemed to us that it led beyond the stars. The things themselves would take some explaining but it was not beyond possibility that they were some subterranean form of terrestrial being, however loathsome and malignant to our eyes and senses.

My brain was occupied with these and other unproductive thoughts as we lurched and staggered along the endless corridor, back towards the comforting presence of our colleagues. We were not far from them when we heard the scream.

3

How can I describe it at this distance in time? I hesitate to use the term but it had such a horrific quality, as if whoever uttered it, had his soul torn from his body. The quavering echoes of this hideous intrusion had not yet died away along the corridors before scream after scream came to companion it. My legs buckled and

I must assuredly have fallen had Scarsdale not got his strong hand under my elbow. I muttered some apology, trying to conceal the trembling in my limbs. I hoped Scarsdale was not disappointed in my qualities as a man of action; he had expected so much but the conditions we were meeting here were so bizarre and the occurrences so outside the range of normal experience that I feared I was making but a sorry showing. Yet he seemed to have noticed nothing, merely quickened his pace into a jog-trot and the pair of us continued to trundle the trolley along the endless tunnels.

The screams had died out now and were not repeated but there came only the low crackle of atmospherics as I jerkily called Van Damm on the radio over and over again. I heard the faint reports of a revolver then; Scarsdale heard them too. He grunted deep down in his throat.

"That sounded like Holden's voice," he said grimly. "The scream, I mean. The things have apparently got round by side tunnels. I hope Van Damm has managed to hold his own. Holden was certainly in no fit state to help."

"We shall be there in a few minutes," I said. "Do you think we ought to leave the trolley and rejoin the others?"

"God, no," said Scarsdale with an intensity I had never heard in his voice before. "That would be fatal. Remember, whatever happens, to stay by the trolley. It holds the grenades and other heavy armaments. They are our only hope if any more of these things appear."

We had slackened our pace somewhat by now, as the weight of the trolley was beginning to tell at this speed. We shuffled together, neither speaking, my mind filled with unnameable dread as the light gradually began to lose its strength along the tunnel. We knew then that we must be nearing the spot where we had left our two companions. The radio was still emitting its sizzling static but there were no responses to the calls I continued to make every five minutes or so. Instinctively, Scarsdale and I switched on our helmet lights and with the yellow radiance burning comfortably ahead of us, completed the last stage of our journey.

I myself now had a deep loathing of the dark tunnels and I fought to keep control as I thought of the long miles of corridor along which we must pass over many days if we were to regain the sanity of the outer air. It seemed to have taken us months to penetrate this far and until we could rejoin the tractors we would stand little chance on foot against our lumbering opponents. I gave thanks for the fact that we had first encountered them in the brilliant light of space as my sanity must inevitably have tottered had they burst upon us in the inky-blackness of the outer mountains or in the twilight which now reigned about us.

Though they had apparently reached Van Damm and Holden by a circuitous route I was by no means certain in my own mind that this was so. The creatures were apparently emerging into the underground complex from the Great White Space and, unless they had incredible restraint, did not inhabit the city of Croth or the long labyrinth which separated us from the outer world, or we would surely have seen signs of them long ago.

It was true, as Scarsdale had suggested, that they might well have means of coming up behind us. But equally Holden, with his strained nerves and now the breakdown of his physical health, might have screamed during medical treatment. This did not explain Van Damm's continued silence but there was just a slim chance that he might have noticed something unusual and gone off to investigate. These were the rationalisations I presented to myself as we panted down the last stretch of tunnel which separated us from our companions.

That they were not logical or sequential thoughts did not matter. I myself was partly unhinged with terror, even if only temporarily; Prescott's sudden and shocking death would have been enough for that – and my reaction to that was to feverishly assure my inner self that there could be a rational – even an ordinary explanation for anything which happened, however extraordinary it might appear to the outward eye. I had just reached this point in my rambling evaluation when Scarsdale gave a grunt and pulled at my arm. We both stopped the trolley as if at a given command and automatically stepped behind it. We had reached the point where we had left our companions. Apart from the crackle of the radio, now that the rumble of the trolley wheels had ceased, an unnatural silence pervaded the miles of tunnel that stretched about us.

Eighteen

I

Again, I must be perfectly precise in the words I now choose to lay the terrible facts of the Great Northern Expedition before the public. We were, as I have said, almost at the point where we had left Van Damm and Holden. The first thing we saw in the glimmer of our helmet lamps was the glint of several small objects lying upon the hard floor of the tunnel. Both Scarsdale and I had our revolvers out by this time, of course, and as I was farthest from the tunnel wall I walked in front of the trolley and bent down to examine our find.

I picked up several used cartridge cases. I handed them to Scarsdale without a word.

"Those were the shots we heard," said Scarsdale grimly, putting the spent shells in his pocket. "He had time to re-load, then."

We pushed on the remaining few yards with the trolley; there were several debouching tunnels from the main corridor at this point and we kept a sharp look-out. It was I who first noticed the sickening stench which grew stronger as we proceeded. I had a hard time to keep a firm grip on my nerves and if it had not been for Scarsdale's sturdy presence I might well have given way to flight.

He, without any outward sign of emotion, merely motioned me to stop the trolley and in his bull-like voice sent echoing shouts along the corridor. As their wandering reverberations died away along the miles of caverns, we listened in vain for any reply from Holden or Van Damm. After a few more shouts which were answered by a faint scuttering noise from somewhere far off and which caused me to tighten my grip on the butt of my revolver, Scarsdale and I heaved and shouldered the crippled trolley the final hundred feet.

We had left some stores at this point, including a stretcher, on which had reposed the blanketed form of Holden. What we first saw on the tunnel floor now was the tumbled and disarrayed blankets and then the stretcher itself, turned upside down and from it ran a trail of the slime-like excretion we had seen already in the ancient city of Croth. I felt my throat constrict with fear but before I could voice any opinion both Scarsdale and I, at almost the identical moment, sighted Holden.

To my intense relief he appeared to be all right; he had apparently fainted – perhaps with shock at the sudden drama which had caused Van Damm to fire? He was half-seated on one of the small packing crates we had stacked against the wall of the tunnel, his shoulder resting on the wall and his head sunk on to his chest as if he were too tired to hold it up any longer. Letting go the trolley I bounded forward and put my hand on my friend's arm to arouse him. Scarsdale's shouted warning came too late. Although it happened years ago that moment of frozen horror is with me now.

For the figure of Holden, wafer-thin and insubstantial as a husk from which all the living goodness had been drained, as a leech ingests the blood of its victim, turned from the wall with a harsh paper-like rustle. It twisted in my hand and the horrified face of Holden, perfect in all its detail as to hair and eyes and skin, began to buckle and disintegrate in the wavering yellow light of my lantern while all the time there came a high, shrill scream from the slightly parted lips, like the hiss of escaping air.

And hideously and inexorably the disembowelled shell that once was Holden twisted and collapsed like the nauseous bag of wind and tissue that it was and the flabby, sac-like thing was finally reduced to a grey, shrivelled bag of skin no bigger than my fist which would assuredly have blown away along the corridor had there been any wind to carry it. All that remained, apart from a hank of hair, the shrivelled skin and the clothes, were the ten toenails and the ten fingernails of our friend.

I myself descended into shrieking, gibbering madness then and it was only half an hour later that I came to myself, after Scarsdale had literally slapped me into sensibility. I came round to find myself propped against the wall of the tunnel with the bearded form of Scarsdale above me. He was pouring raw brandy down

my throat and as I coughed and puked my way back to conscious-
ness, I saw him gulp a tot of the raw spirit down his own throat.
Otherwise he seemed as strong and imperturbable as ever, as he
lifted me solicitously and helped me into a standing position. I
found my revolver thrust back into my hand while Scarsdale said
over and over again in my ear, as one might to a drowning man,
"Everything is all right, my dear fellow. Everything is all right."

He repeated the words slowly and simply as though the sense
of them might take some time to penetrate – as indeed it did – and
as if the simple repetition might, of itself, be sufficient to dispel the
black nightmare of horror in which we now found ourselves.

For there was worse to follow and it was only over the next hour,
as I calmed and Scarsdale's words began to make more sense, that
I realised we must go back yet again. Back into those tunnels of
abomination toward the region of the Great White Space, where
lurked the insubstantial monadelphous creatures whose bleating
cry we had such cause to fear. But as my nerves recovered and I
grew stronger I realised that Scarsdale was right. Van Damm was
alive – or had been but a short while before – and assuredly needed
our help.

I retched again as I thought of what he might even now be suffering and this in itself underpinned my resolve. Assisted by the
raw spirit I again found my strength and I believe myself to have
been in those last hours once again the man Scarsdale had taken
me for long ago in that far-off tea room by the British Museum;
in another world, another age it now seemed to me. For as I lay
in babbling madness Scarsdale had again heard shots far off down
the tunnel, back in the direction from which we had come and had
then heard Van Damm's choked cry for help.

Knowing him as I did I believe he would have set off alone at
that instant, armed only with his revolver and a few rounds of
ammunition, had it not been for leaving me helpless and unpro-
tected in that spot. In which case I should assuredly have joined
Holden and Prescott in death; I owe Scarsdale my life not once
but many times and though the gift of existence has become a
tortured burden to me in these latter years, I did not then know to
what I would latterly be reduced and I was brimming full of grati-

tude and hope during the first few minutes of my newly recovered sanity, before I was fully cognisant that we must return.

Yet, when my senses were fully restored, I was as eager as Scarsdale to see what we could do to effect the rescue of the unfortunate Van Damm. Would not I have been demented had I been in Van Damm's position and imagined that we knew he was alive and were doing nothing to attempt his rescue? We had to go; I knew this as well as Scarsdale and I soon made him see that I realised the duty we owed to our tragic companion. He clapped me silently on the shoulder and then we set to to assess the situation.

First, we prepared a quick meal and ate it as we stripped down the trolley; it was many hours since we had eaten and we would be worse than useless if we did not keep up our strength. It was unlikely that the ten minutes we spent on this would make much difference either way but even if it had we could not have prepared ourselves more quickly as we had to discard many items from the trolley's load in order to make better speed.

Reluctantly, we discarded the elephant guns. They had made little impression on the jelly-creatures and were taking up disproportionate weight in the small vehicle which, with one twisted axle, was now extremely awkward to manoeuvre with such a heavy load as we had been carrying.

Too late, we wished we had more Very flares and more grenades; the latter, more than anything seemed to be effective, though of course, neither of us really knew whether the creatures could be killed or even temporarily stopped. I myself felt that fire might be the answer; if we had petrol here we might have made a small lake and, leading the creatures on to it, have ignited the fuel by lobbing grenades into it. But there was no chance of that; we had no petrol so it was useless to speculate further on such lines. There were but two dozen grenades left and we would have to make effective use of them. So, the trolley lightened, Scarsdale and I looked meaningly at one another and for the second time set back along the tunnel for the Great White Space and the outer corridors of hell.

2

The light slowly grew and the throbbing pulsations with it. Scarsdale and I walked purposefully but with all our senses anaesthetised; neither of us cared to talk of the fears haunting the edges of our minds. Indeed, we hardly dared hint even to ourselves what might be waiting in the slowly growing light at the end of the tunnel. We had heard or seen nothing in the ten minutes since we had started. The going was uphill again but the trolley was lighter now and giving no trouble, though it was making more noise than either of us would have liked.

Both of us had checked the revolvers hanging at our belts; my pockets were stuffed with cartridges and two Very pistols sat on the load in the trolley, near to my hand. Scarsdale's belt seemed to bristle with weapons; strangely enough, I had forgotten to ask him where he had obtained his most bizarre find. This was an old naval cutlass in a brass and leather scabbard which now jogged reassuringly at his hip. Strangely enough, this museum piece might be more useful to us than a machine-gun in face of our weird adversaries.

Had our companions been issued with them, there might have been a very different outcome to the past twelve hours. Though who could have foreseen such creatures; even Scarsdale, with his greater knowledge, could not have imagined such beings. I preferred myself to keep them firmly within my mind as natural phenomena existing within the subterranean depths of the earth. I could not grasp the mathematical complexities involved in assuming that somehow, space could be bent so that a door to the stars could exist many miles below the surface of the earth. Scarsdale could have spent weeks with a blackboard and chalk and I should have been none the wiser. But I was slowly coming round to the idea, as horrifying and outrageous as it might appear.

The light grew and my thoughts, despite my resolve to keep a blank mind, constantly revolved around such suppositions as our progress gradually took us back into the area of strengthening light. The pulsations grew also and then we had crossed the old slime-trails of our previous penetration. Like Scarsdale I had tied a handkerchief around my throat and I now put it across my nose and mouth to blot out some of the nauseous stench. The goggles were pushed up to my forehead and I lowered the smoked glass over my eyes as white fingers of extra-terrestrial origin began to probe at the far distance.

Scarsdale and I had prepared earplugs of cotton wool on this occasion and with these in position we were somewhat insulated from reality, as both felt we must be if we were to survive. But the lessening of our sensibilities which this would imply, particularly of hearing and sight, carried its own dangers and the Professor and I had previously arranged that each would protect the other's back in an emergency.

We stopped the trolley where the ghastly pulsating brilliance of the ever-increasing light source beat upon the floor of the corridor like a physical flood. We had piled the grenades into a wicker basket which had once contained batteries for our generators and each taking a handle we carried it between us, leaving the other hand free for the revolvers. Despite the plugs and goggles the intensity of the light source combined with the insidious beat of the unknown pulse induced a sense of nausea in me as we at last came out on the great disc of glowing radiance that Scarsdale had christened – so aptly – The Great White Space.

Nothing stirred, there was no movement in the far shadows behind but newly-created slime-trails described whorled patterns on the rock floor before us.

Both of us dropped to the ground, despite the increased stench here, and tried to make what we could of this enigmatic trail. The surface of the corridor, of course, was too hard to carry any impression such as might be made by the dragging heels of Van Damm's recumbent figure but the trails did tell us something. They went, not as we had feared, directly towards the pale oval of white-hot luminosity that vibrated and throbbed in time to the drum-beat but curved off to one side; a rocky spur projected here and led to an area of shadow, farther back, and beyond the rim of the pale fire of space.

Dragging the trolley behind us, Scarsdale and I made our way

over, cautiously glancing behind and to either side. As we gained
the shadowed area the stench became more unbearable. It was like
an open, suppurating wound from a patient suffering from some
loathsome disease. Even Scarsdale seemed affected and I could see
beads of moisture glittering in his beard and running down in rivu-
lets across his chin. We now had our backs to the white luminosity
and had to adjust our eyes to the greatly changed conditions.

There was a narrow shelf of rock on which we now stood; both
of us seized a couple of grenades and put them in our pockets in
case of emergency. We pulled the trolley as close in to the shelf
as possible, in case we had to leave in a hurry and walked across
the entrances of three dark caverns which were now materialising
from the gloom.

We both saw Van Damm's hunched form at the same time;
abandoning precaution we were about to run forward when I put
my hand on Scarsdale's shoulder and arrested our hasty action.
With my recent horrifying experience fresh in my mind I had no
wish to repeat the ordeal; both Scarsdale and I by now thought
it extremely unlikely that our unfortunate companion could have
survived. There was a bare chance, of course. Van Damm was lying
with his face to the rock wall; except that he was on the ground
the posture was hideously reminiscent of Holden. I had no desire
to see Van Damm's inanimate figure collapse in disintegrating ruin
and for that reason my feet remained resolutely fast to the floor of
the cavern.

But it was not so much Van Damm as a small, furtive movement
in the dimness which had caught the corner of my eye and registered itself as a minute flicker. I directed my companion's gaze
towards it and we both removed our goggles. I had difficulty in
preventing myself from screaming; I now saw that a long tube of
some grey-coloured material stretched from beneath Van Damm's
collapsed body. It led back several yards to the edge of one of the
cave entrances.

Round the corner was peering one of the most hideous visages
it has ever been my misfortune to encounter, even in the grip of
nightmare. The creature's face was grey; it slobbered from slit-
like mouth and red-rimmed nostrils and it was this which gave

off the nauseating slime which littered the floor of the caves. The eyes were large, jelly-like plates covered by some form of pulsating membrane, which pulsed and glowed so that at one moment the lids were opaque and at the next the greenish-tinged core of the eye was staring through. The ears were pointed and bat-like; yellowed and crooked teeth glinted among the slime in its mouth.

The grey tube grew into an elephant-like proboscis which waved slowly about as the thing sucked or pumped fluids either out or into Van Damm's body. Neither of us could make out which and I was as near collapse as I had been at any time during this expedition. Mercifully, I could not see any more of the creature, the bulk of which was hidden beyond the cave entrance but it could not have been less than fifty feet high. It had a scaly claw which it used to probe the surface of the tube from time to time. I did not think it had seen us, for some obscure reason, and Scarsdale and I each took the pin out of a grenade.

Then, as I moved slowly forward my foot scraped on a projection in the tunnel floor; this seemed to disturb the nightmare being and as it turned to face us, I heard again the strange rustling I had heard so long ago at the entrance to these caves of madness. The thing had great leathery wings, in a transparent casing on its shoulders and these brushed together as it moved. The tube was withdrawn with lightning rapidity; whip-like, it snaked back along the floor. Scarsdale and I had each thrown a grenade by this time; the second set followed while the first were in the air. We flung ourselves down as scarlet flame spurted in the gloom and fragments of metal went whanging viciously about the cavern. Above the crackle of charred flesh as we rolled back along the floor into the light, was a high, bleating moan which seemed to penetrate my eardrums, even with the cotton wool plugs.

I looked up, rigid with shock. The moan was now mingled with shrill, urgent screams; then I saw beyond the writhing horror of the winged creature, the flabby slobbing figures of the monadelphous things and their urgent bleating sounded above the crackle of flame. Scarsdale had rolled back to the trolley and got off two more grenades as I rose and went over to the form of Van Damm.

I was prepared now for what I saw but the shock was, if anything, far greater than that of my experience with Holden.

Perhaps we had interrupted the bat creature at a crucial moment of the metamorphosis or possibly the process was a long and elaborate one. I was prepared for anything but the ruined mask of Van Damm's dead features which confronted me. Poor Van Damm's lower jaw had been quite torn off in some disgusting manner, exposing the upper teeth and splintered bone of the jaw connections with long driblets of blackened blood hanging down from the ruin. More disgustingly still, the skull had been opened in some ingenious manner – perhaps with a cutting tool on the bat creature's trunk – and the brainbox exposed.

Mercifully, I had no time to linger over this nauseating sight because of Scarsdale's shouted warning and then a whole wave of the bleating jelly-things were upon us and I was too busy pulling grenade pins, hurling, retreating and then surging forward again so that the incidents of the next half hour became a vague, confused jumble in my mind. Mingled with the physical weariness was a hard, burning anger at the obscenities we were confronting, so that in a strange way unknown to myself, I lost all fear.

We were insulated from the noise, of course, by our helmets and the ear-plugs which was just as well, as the din as the explosions rolled reverberating down miles of corridor must have been tremendous. The creatures, for all their agility and hopping-motion got in each other's way because of their vast size so that we seemed to create a giant slaughter in that corner of the cavern.

But curiously we never found a single corpse of the jelly-beings; the bat-like creature was different and that cadaver had soon assumed a blue putrescence and gradually shrivelled away. We found only patches of slime upon the ground after each fresh encounter with the hopping monstrosities; they seemed to help one another with their little hands and tendrils and more than once, as the battle raged over the central area which led to the throbbing vacancy of the Great White Space, we saw those not wounded assisting others seriously disabled back into the pulsating brilliance, where they disappeared from our sight.

At last, when we had only a few grenades left, they drew off and an awful silence descended. Scarsdale and I found ourselves dirty, smoke-grimed, perspiring and utterly weary in a slime-crusted arena marked only by the long tracks where we had dragged the trolley around behind us. Eyes narrowed to slits beneath the dark goggles we gazed achingly towards the burning whiteness which led to outer space; nothing moved in that vile phosphorescence and the only movements were our own; the only sound the faint scrape of our own footfall.

We retreated slowly, withdrawing two or three hundred yards down the corridor, into a mercifully more shadowed area where we crouched behind the trolley, and, on Scarsdale assuming the office of sentry, debated our position. There was little, or nothing we could now do; three of our companions had been killed – though as yet our tired minds could not comprehend the enormity of this loss. Our primary duty was now to ourselves and to the world. There was no further choice; Scarsdale, in his own mind, I am certain, had contemplated penetrating even the vastness of The Great White Space and had our way not been initially barred by the creatures he would have pushed on – with or without the rest of us. That course was denied us and all that remained was to extricate ourselves without incurring any further danger, make our way back to civilisation and warn the world of what we had witnessed.

"We must gather our strength," said Scarsdale. "I will take the first watch while you get some rest."

He was still the leader but even as I denied being tired the truth was that I was exhausted mentally and physically. Though his robust frame and phlegmatic exterior made it difficult to believe, I felt also that Scarsdale himself was very near to breaking point. Neither of us was in a fit state to walk more than a few hundred yards let alone be in a posture to beat off a further attack.

We had to have rest and the safest and most obvious course, in the comparatively secure part of the tunnel to which we had retreated was for each to sleep for an hour. Then we would be able to carry on in a relatively refreshed condition. Scarsdale had no sooner pressed his point than I felt a great heaviness on my eyelids. I laid my head upon my hands and slept.

Nineteen

I

When I awoke I had at first difficulty in remembering where I was. It seemed dark and almost impossible to see. My throat too was dry and dusty and I was conscious of an aching in all my limbs. I had not eaten for some time and was beginning to feel the faint stirrings of hunger. I had fallen sideways, I found, and was now lying with my head against the side wall of the tunnel. As soon as I was fully awake I at once became aware of the horror of the situation.

I struggled immediately into a sitting position, the breath rasping in my throat. I had somewhat foolishly left my goggles in situ and I now found, when I had removed them, that there were deep grooves cut into my forehead and the back of my neck. But of course I could now see quite clearly in the faint light and my eyes first fell upon the trolley with its twisted axle, which had nevertheless served us so well.

I pulled myself slowly upright by its metal framework, shocked to discover how exhausted I was. There was a trembling in all my limbs and a momentary dizziness in front of my eyes, which I put down to the reaction to the events of the past few hours. I supported myself by one hand against the tunnel wall and as my vision cleared I became aware of the extreme quietness in this portion of the tunnel. At the same time I saw Scarsdale's revolver lying on the ground at the spot where I had last seen him.

The shock was as vivid as a douche of cold water in my face and I was suddenly awake, my raw nerves fretting afresh, a nameless fear tugging at the corners of my mind. I had imagined that Scarsdale had been sitting on the other side of the trolley, his back to it and facing down the tunnel towards the source of light and from which any danger must come. At first I was almost too concerned and worried to take the few steps necessary to confirm or dispel my fears.

It took a considerable effort of will to move. I had my revolver out now and holding it in front of me and with my other hand hooked over the rail of the trolley I edged round. I expected some horrific sight and relief flooded over me when I became aware that the space behind the trolley was filled with nothing more tangible than shadow. Professor Scarsdale was not there. But this fact, coupled with the unusual circumstance of the revolver lying on the ground, had assumed its true significance by this time. The realisation that all could not be well stung like acid and seemed to sear my nerves making me at once both wide awake and half-frantic with worry.

I was immediately drenched with varying emotions and ran back up the tunnel toward the strengthening light, calling for the Professor. Nothing answered except the hideous echoes of my own voice which seemed to reverberate along aching miles of tunnel towards the infinitely remote entrance to this abode of despair beneath the Black Mountains. My fear of the slug-creatures was momentarily submerged in my greater terror at being left entirely alone in this abomination.

I dare not dwell on the suppositions which this released, lest my sanity might totter and I ran up and down the passage for several minutes, quite demented. Then, coming to myself and pressing my trembling hands together I forced my shrieking nerves into calmness. I could only assume that some harm had befallen Scarsdale or he would have replied to my shouts; or, he might perhaps have decided to explore the farther regions of the Great White Space on his own, beyond earshot. Or, thirdly, he was already past all human aid. By this slow and laboured reasoning did I seek to calm my nerves. There was a fourth possibility; that he had gone back along the tunnel in the opposite direction but this I immediately discounted. It was against all our reasoning – unless something alien or unusual had appeared in that direction.

I put that from me. There remained the unmistakable, indeed inescapable, fact that I had to go back towards the Great White Space. Alive or dead Scarsdale had to be found. And there was only me left to either rescue Scarsdale from the same abominable fate which had overtaken our companions or, tragic thought, to vindicate his memory. When I had come to this conclusion I became calmer, stopped my pacing about and checked my revolver and ammunition; I seized a canvas bag and putting the remaining five grenades in it set off back up the tunnel.

2

I had walked only a few hundred yards when I became aware of a low, muttered mumbling up ahead. The light was growing in intensity now or my courage might perhaps have failed me, so I merely gripped the bag more firmly and went on. I could not at first place the direction from which the sound was coming. At one moment it resembled the faint buzz of insects, such as one might hear on a hot summer day in happier circumstances, when hovering on the edge of sleep.

But the idea of insects in the connotation of these repellent underground caverns was abhorrent in the extreme and my resolution took a hard knock at the outset. The faint mumble seemed to recede and advance like the waves of the sea as I went down the corridor of ever-strengthening light and I donned my goggles in order that they should be ready when the radiance became too strong for my naked eyes. The insidious murmur now resembled a human being whispering some obscene thought in one of the caves almost beyond earshot and that was even more unpleasant, if anything.

But conversely, I felt my courage reviving. Might not Scarsdale have suffered some accident and even now, on hands and knees, be trying to make his way back to me, muttering some plea for help? This thought made me suck in my breath with an audible sound and life seemed to flow into my limbs; I went on down the corridor at a jog-trot.

The light grew stronger, washing in like surf over the black walls of the caves. There was no sign of Scarsdale; nothing moved in the whole of the corridor before me but the mumbling buzz grew in my ears, not at all overborne by the throbbing vibrations of the great pulse which were now again growing in intensity. I made sure I had my ear-plugs handy and switched off the lamp in my helmet. I was not sure how long these batteries lasted and I would need the light for the return.

I dared not think too closely of my returning without Scarsdale; that was a horror which did not bear contemplation in the circumstances in which I now found myself placed. My breath whistled uneasily in my throat as I hurried uphill, the grenades making an unpleasant clicking noise as they bounced together in the canvas holder in my left hand.

My right hand held the revolver poised but despite the rigid grip of my fingers round the butt and trigger guard I could not stop the trembling in my fingers. Strange convention that impelled me still to cling to such a traditional weapon as a firearm. We had all seen how ineffective they had proved in our abortive battles with the slug-creatures, yet training was so ingrained that one clung to habit even where it had been proved useless. Thus I proved to myself that not only scientists cling uselessly to empiricism. Though of course scientists would then change their methods, whereas I was still clinging literally and pointlessly to mine.

So I reasoned jerkily to myself as I pounded onwards into the strengthening light, prepared for anything as I neared the slight curve of the corridor which cut me off from sight of the approaches to the Great White Space, while all the while the mumbled mutter of the hidden whisperers grew with the thudding pulse in my ears.

As I rounded the slight curve the pulsations grew markedly stronger and the intensity of the light to drastically undergo a change. The paleness turned from an opaque milkiness to the sharp brilliance of sunshine and then as I came suddenly out into the featureless arena where the walls of the caves fell away altogether the light seemed to dazzle my eyeballs and a pale thunderclap sounded in my ears. I clamped the goggles down over my eyes at once and as I staggered, smitten with the tremendous strength of the shafts of luminescence, the whispering hissed at my elbow as though the unknown mumblers were only a foot or so from where I stood.

I put in the ear-plugs as the throbbing grew to intolerable proportions. I was now bathed in liquid phosphorescence so bright that even my arms seemed to be lapped with living fire and so incandescent that the extremities of my limbs had disappeared.

I narrowed my eyes to slits as I ran on and reached for the first grenade. It was like peering into a seething cauldron; the Great White Space was alive with throbbing pulsations of living light and through this blanched hole which led into the universe hopped and lurched not only the flopping slug-things we had earlier encountered but the living counterparts of the creatures we had seen in the jars.

They were far off and appeared not to have seen me as they flowed in a ghastly stream in and out of the luminescent circle on their obscure errands. But what took my eye and filled me with unutterable relief was the sight of the durable figure of Scarsdale. He stood to one side, almost in the spot where we had the last battle with the things in the side-galleries. His beard glowed with living fire as he waved and gestured to me excitedly.

"Coming, Scarsdale," I said, relief surging through me. My words echoed and boomed through the galleries and disturbed the hopping things that crowded in and out of that horrifying door into space. They hesitated, broke ranks and once again that vile bleating and lowing noise echoed under the arch of the caverns. I took the pin out of a grenade and held it tightly. I altered course and ran toward Scarsdale. He hobbled up to meet me and I was worried that he might be injured but he continued to wave reassuringly.

There was now about a hundred yards separating us but the slug-creatures, half-seen from the corner of my eye were rapidly closing halfway between the two of us.

"Hurry, Professor," I called. "We shall be cut off."

The burly form of Scarsdale continued to wave.

"There is no danger, Plowright," he called back. "I have made the most fantastic discoveries."

As I got closer to him I saw a surge of the winged insect-like creatures appear from the rock galleries behind him. Once again came the leathery beat of the horny wing-cases which had so haunted my dreams.

"Behind you," I called, anxiety blurring the edges of my voice. I turned on my heel abruptly and hurled my grenade into the mass of hopping things which were crowding through the Great White

Space to separate the two of us. The bleating cries changed to those of alarm as the grenade rolled onwards. The explosion made a sharp bang which slapped at the sides of the cavern, red flame bloomed, darkening the brilliance of white light and angry pieces of metal buzzed vindictively about. There were again the moans of distress and the stench of scorched tissue but more and more of the flabby creatures, their bundled tentacles groping and writhing, were coming on. I threw three grenades rapidly with the strength of desperation and before the first explosion slapped back from the cave walls I was halfway across the distance which separated me from Scarsdale.

By now several of the things were almost level with the pair of us and still coming on, slopping across the cave floor with incredible speed. I called again to the Professor to make haste but he seemed to be slowing now, as though he were exhausted.

The horrible stench, which had been ever present, was now intensified and again I narrowed my eyes to slits as the pulsations of white light appeared to ululate to the rhythmic beat of those devilish vibrations. I glimpsed the forms of the slug-things all about me now, their monadelphous outlines fibrillating and undulating in the pitiless glare from outer space. Behind them I caught sight of one or two of the winged beasts, who seemed to be balefully directing the activities of the others.

But I was now almost up to Scarsdale and there was still a wide patch of cave floor which would give us a means of escape back to the blessed dimness of the caverns, if only we had the few more seconds necessary. I made a last despairing spurt and Scarsdale, glancing up, gave me a smile of encouragement and welcome. Uselessly I had my revolver in my left hand and took the opportunity to get off two or three shots into the air. I did not even bother to aim at the slug things as I knew the effect of the bullets on them would be less than useless.

But the creatures paused in their bleating progress just long enough for me to reach him. He tottered as I caught him by the arm and swung him to face me.

"Thank God, I was in time, Professor," I panted. "We have only a few seconds."

He shook his head.

"You don't understand, Plowright," he said. "We are on the verge of the most incredible discoveries."

The slug-creatures started to slop forward again as he spoke. I felt irritation lancing through my brain but I forced myself to keep calm. This was no time for the scientific mind to become predominant.

"We are in mortal danger, Professor," I shouted, not noticing that he was without his ear-plugs. "Why did you not wake me?"

I pulled him back behind me, towards the welcoming shade of the inner passages. He did not resist; indeed, he seemed almost without will, as though his latest investigations had temporarily exhausted him.

The glare from the Great White Space made everything look blanched and strange but the Professor's attitude alarmed me; there was something about his head which was not quite right. He looked ill and somehow crumpled. Perhaps he had been attacked by the creatures and was still suffering from injuries. He kept his head turned away from me as if his neck hurt him. I saw stickiness on his clothing then. My vision blurred and I slipped on the unspeakable foulness of that unholy floor.

I pulled Scarsdale again and he broke into a shambling run beside me.

"Quickly, Professor," I shouted, "or we shall be too late."

He nodded then as if he understood. But just at that moment some of the slug-creatures, who were getting dangerously close, came up towards us. They mewed with that strange, distressing call and the whole air seemed to be filled with that unearthly vibrancy.

Scarsdale had slowed his pace again as if he were waiting for them.

"You do not understand, Plowright," he said again. "There are fantastic things to be learned here, if only one has the courage. I must tell you. I beg you not to resist further."

I did not understand him and turned round, keeping my grip on his arm.

Three of the slug-things were quite close now and moved hesitantly toward me, as though they sensed the dangers of the last grenade in my hand. When I looked back at Scarsdale he once again had his head averted.

"Are you injured, Professor?" I said.

He shook his head. I removed my eyes from him once more and then turned again to the menacing line of things that were spread out in front of us. They waved their tendrils slowly, their forms half-transparent in the brilliant light. I glanced at the group nearest to me and then my knees buckled and there came an uncontrollable trembling in my limbs. I glanced wildly over my shoulder, saw my retreat was clear into the blessed darkness.

Scarsdale smiled at me encouragingly and then it happened. I glanced stupefied from him to the slug-things and then I shrieked and shrieked as though I would never stop. I tasted the bitter taste of blood and bile in my mouth and my brain was a seething cauldron of white-hot terror. I hurled the Professor from me and, with the mewing cries of the slug-things vibrating in my ears and with that unutterable stench in my nostrils I fled from the Great White Space and plunged headlong into the tunnels for my life.

Twenty

I

I fled as though from nightmare. I ran until the breath was throbbing in my throat and the brilliance of The Great White Space had faded to the dim luminosity of the farther corridors. Once or twice I must have cannoned into the walls because I later found my clothing torn and blood on my hands and finger-nails. At some point I had the good sense to switch on my helmet lamp and its bright yellow beam sliced and bobbed along the corridor like a beckoning finger.

Mercifully, I had dropped the remaining hand grenade and my pistol or I might have done myself an injury in my horrified and agitated condition. My head was a red-hot furnace, perspiration dripped down my face and I reeled and lurched like a man in fever.

It was not until some time had passed that I thought to remove my goggles and then I hurled them behind me. I found myself back at the trolley but so great was my fear and the shrieking state of my nerves that I dare not stop there.

My mind could not encompass the immensity of the journey which faced me so I thought only of getting through the next few hours; of surviving until then, when I would try to make plans. At least, I reasoned this out later; for my knowledge of the events while they were taking place is muddled and blurred. There was food on the trolley; I knew that. There were weapons and Very flares too; those meant survival, life and the sanity of the outside world. At that moment I cared not whether I lived or died but if I died at least let it be with the sweet skies of the outer earth above me and the kiss of the sun on my face.

I longed for the fresh breezes of the upper earth and was terrified of dying like a rat in a hole down here, miles beneath the surface. So somehow, though normally I would have thought it beyond my strength at that time, I manhandled the trolley, defective and difficult to wheel as it was, and set off in the southward direction. Every so often I would stop and listen with straining ears for the faintest scratch of a footfall, the rasp of leathery wings or the sinister whispering that would have been the sign that I was pursued. My sanity hung by a thread at those moments and I would not, for all the money in the world, endure the tortures I endured during those next few days.

Indeed my cheeks were sunken like an old man and my hair a shade or two whiter when I eventually ended my ordeal. But there was nothing moving in all the long corridors behind me; the warm wind blew from the north and the faint pulse, hourly growing feebler, again pumped out its sinister message. I put the sound at my back and it gradually died away though it persisted for many a long mile, just as it had on the inward journey.

Mercifully, I had a small compass on me with which I could make sure I was homing southwards, for in my mental state and in the delirium which followed, I would surely have gone blindly back in the northward direction without it. My remaining portable camera too, supported on its strap round my neck, was banging against the walls as I pushed, until at last I took it off and laid it down on the trolley.

The few shots in the camera itself and a dozen or so prints I had in an envelope and which had been brought with us from the tractor-base were the only things I was to bring out from the Great Northern Expedition intact, and the manner of losing the others I will speak of later. That first day I remained more or less coherent, though my physical condition gradually deteriorated. I was drenched in perspiration and the wind blowing on my back, warm as it was, must have set up a feverish condition as my skin was icy cold.

At some time – I had long ago forgotten whether the hour on my wrist watch indicated day or night – I slumped down and ate a meal from the tinned provisions on the trolley. I was so far coherent at that stage, that I was able to sort out some of the stores. By jettisoning the heavier containers and a few of the more bulky elephant guns and weapons of that sort, I managed to lighten the load considerably. My biggest dread, something which gnawed constantly at the edges of my mind, was that the creatures would cut round behind me, through interconnecting caves, just as they must have done with poor Holden and Van Damm. I did not dare dwell on this overlong; but mercifully, I found a bottle of whisky on the trolley and swigged a good quarter of it, so that my mind must have been deadened and dulled about this time.

There was no sign of pursuit, thank God, and as the hours passed I began to feel a little more security in my mind; of course, this may well have been due to the blunting of my sensibilities with the liquor but whatever the cause, I thanked the Almighty for it. In this way I suppose I must have covered a considerable distance before I finally slumped down and sleep mercifully took me.

2

I went on running. No-one came after me. Despite intense questioning from many eminent authorities in the field, I was never able to give any consequential explanation of my movements or explain coherently how many days it took me to regain civilisation again. Neither could I pinpoint the time when I finally broke down and fever claimed me. The dates between my re-appearance in the valley before the Black Mountains and my arrival at what cynics may describe as a "civilised community" was something like six months.

I am told also that I had been in fever for almost two months and if it had not been for the devoted efforts of a French doctor and a German nursing sister I should assuredly have died. Perhaps, under the stress of these dreary after days, it might have been better so. But I am drawing ahead of my narrative. I made my way onwards, still pushing the trolley, guiding myself by compass. I must have taken my meals automatically from the provisions in the cases, for I have no clear recollection after all this time of how I ate or what I ate.

I could have had no formal routine and with my unkempt beard, wild, staring eyes, and haggard features I must have made an appalling sight for those who found me. But somehow, I made out along those hellish corridors until I at last found myself among features with which I had already become familiar. Truly, there is a providence which looks after fools and eventually, tired, sick and half-hysterical with the fading remembrance of the terrifying events through which I had passed, I at length found myself once more within the desolate City of Croth.

The river, dank and sombre as the Styx, with its weird bridge was passed safely and shortly after this, among the suburbs, I must have abandoned the trolley which had served me so well. It must be there now, will surely remain there for all eternity, a mute witness to man's incredible folly. For looking back over this vast distance in time since I took part in the fated Great Northern Expedition, I have surmised that it could only have been incredible folly which led us there.

Folly on the part of those who followed so blindly; and incredible folly on the part of the leaders, Van Damm and Scarsdale, who knew quite clearly what dread areas at the rim of human experience into which they were venturing. And yet I can only assume that great wisdom and great scientific knowledge go hand in hand with a mental blindness of a particularly virulent sort. Had any of us the merest inkling of the realities which were waiting at the end of those tunnels, nothing would have brought any of us within a hundred miles of the Black Mountains.

I must have slept from time to time, though I have no knowledge of it; fear was ever at my shoulder, speeding me onwards through the dim luminescence and the weird perspectives of Croth. Here I found further supplies and stores and must have taken what I wanted for sustenance. Of the City itself, apart from the great central square, I recall nothing. Croth and its wonders; its fabulous library and all the teeming treasures of its thousands of fabled years, lies still beneath the pallid glow of those dim and vaporous vaults.

I fled ever onwards. The pulse died away and the dry wind was now at my back, pushing me homewards. I must have stopped, eaten, slept and done a thousand and one other things yet I have still no clear idea how I passed my time. How many days this occupied I know not but from simple calculations I have since conjectured that the journey must have been but a fraction of that spent on the inward trip. Fear gave me strength and sustained me through the long ordeal which brought me close to madness but nothing stirred in the drear miles; the only sounds once the pulse had died away were the pounding of the blood in my head and the dry echo of my own feet rushing headlong through those corridors of eternity.

I eventually came into the more blessed obscurity of the farther caverns, picking up stores as I gained the various caches and depots, tragic reminders now of my colleagues who were no more; discarding other items as being too bulky or past their use. As the days passed and I was not pursued and saw no sign of any pursuer, so my resolve strengthened and with it my physical stamina. I gained the Embalming Gallery, doubly abhorrent to me with the knowledge of what lay within those row upon row of silent jars; my compass I retained and with it mercifully pointed myself towards the south and this, together with a small store of photographs and some food and provisions, was all I carried when I at last reached the underground lake.

Here I fell in an exhausted stupor and must have slept for something like two days and nights; I had no means of recording dates but somehow I retained the presence of mind to re-wind my watch each night and morning and in the intervals of conscious-ness between my bouts of broken sleep I must have re-wound it automatically because I cannot once remember it having ever stopped. Indeed it contributed greatly to my sanity as I more than once woke to its soothing tick alongside my ear as I stretched on hard rock or the yielding sand of the shore.

I bitterly regretted now that I had not been more selective in what I had chosen to take away. If anything had happened to the tractors or I could not start them, I should have to rely on the batteries in my helmet lamp to see myself home. And they would surely be exhausted many, many days before I could tramp the long miles and then should I indeed descend into shrieking insanity. I greatly regretted too not being able to bring back Scars-dale's thumbed notes or his typewritten copy of The Ethics of Ygor, which contained the key to the whole enigma. But they had remained with the Professor on that accursed clearance near The Great White Space and were surely lost for ever more.

It must have been a week or longer after I began my headlong flight when I at last stepped into the rubber boat with my small store of necessaries and paddled myself out into the mist and the strange radiant phosphorescence of that eerie Styx.

It was here, or at some stage during the crossing that I lost or mislaid some of my photographic material; certainly, it appeared that water slopping into the bottom of the boat ruined a number of my precious photographic plates, notably those depicting the slug-creatures we had encountered in our first battle involving myself, Scarsdale and Prescott. I have often wondered since, in the lonely night watches, when the wind keens about the house, whether this was accident or design. Certainly, the possibility of some malignant, extra-terrestrial force exerted by these creatures and which might have power at a distance, had not escaped my mind.

Once on the opposite side of the lake I rested again, as before picking up fresh stores and discarding other material; my brain was still numb and frozen and I took care to drink just enough whisky to keep my mind deadened without affecting my faculties. Even so it was a journey carried out by an automata, functioning through sheer good physical health, motivated only by fear and the desire to survive.

I had hardly dared to hope that the tractors would be undisturbed but there they were, beneath their sheets, each a poignant reminder of the companions I had lost. Automatically, my brain functioning mechanically, I threw switches and animated dynamoes until the caverns once again echoed to the throbbing pulse of the motors. Secure beneath my metallic shell I set back along the tunnels, fortified by the throbbing hum of the machinery and the limpid brilliance of the searchlights.

I went at top speed, without stopping, and eating at the controls; it was a remarkable performance and the concentration required was so fantastic that I doubt if I could ever do it again. When I saw the thin sliver of daylight at the entrance to the Mountains, leading to the blessed outer air, my hands faltered on the controls and I wept.

3

So I live now, a shadow of my former self, companioned only by my old friend Robson, to whom I have related this narrative not once but a hundred times. The night wind keens about the earth and taps at the blind in these latitudes and I live again my experiences on the Great Northern Expedition and I am afraid. I owe my life to certain tribesmen who found my tractor wandering in the desert and who guided me and set me in the right direction for the Plain of Darkness and the welcoming huddle of the town of Nylstrom.

Here I paused only a day and then, guided by emissaries of the Headman, and leaving our spare tractor as payment for his services, I set out once again and at last reached Zak. There the story blurs and dies altogether. I fell very ill there. I have already told something of this; my illness and fever lasted for months and when I at last came to myself I was in the sickbay of a P. and O. liner ploughing its way England bound through the Bay of Biscay.

Of all the equipment with which I had set out only my camera, a few plates and a few personal items remained. But I was alive; that was all that mattered – then.

I live much out of the world; my health is irretrievably wrecked, my nights sleepless, my form spectral. I fear dreaming. Sometimes on moonlight nights I stand at my window and look out at the silver disc riding serenely above the treetops and think it shines down upon the Black Mountains so far away and I cannot repress a shudder at the thought of the blasphemous abominations that lurk beneath.

Latterly the lights in the sky have been seen again; I fear the Coming cannot be long delayed now and my heart is sick for the welfare of mankind. Yet I am not believed, will never be believed, though Robson and a few others scientifically-minded have an inkling of the end. For there must come an end.

Why was I allowed to survive? Who knows? The ways of beings from an alien world are strange to us and beyond mortal comprehension. I have thought about it year on interminably weary year. And I cannot fathom a thousandth part of the complexities involved. But that there are horrors beyond human bearing is an irrefutable fact. Did I not myself see with my own eyes?

Those ponderous, monadelphous forms undulating hideously in the baleful light from The Great White Space. And my former colleagues, even Zalor, smiling devilish smiles of welcome. So that I broke and fled screaming from those blasphemous abodes of hell. Who would not have followed my example?

For there, ingested in some vile and unfathomable manner were my friends Holden, Prescott and Van Damm, ALIVE AND PART OF THE SLUG-CREATURES THEMSELVES! Small wonder my sanity tottered. And as if in answer to Zalor's greeting the great Clark Ashton Scarsdale had bowed and turned his head. And from his features had fallen A WAXEN MASK REVEALING UNKNOW-ABLE BLASPHEMIES BENEATH!

As God is my witness I swear this is the truth. I had not realised their essence had been removed for a purpose. But what made the doctors fear for my sanity was the supposition at the back of my mind which almost overturned my reason. For the question has been with me since then and is even more persistent of late. The waxen mask was so plausible in its perfection, so brilliant in its personification of Professor Clark Ashton Scarsdale, that it brings other possibilities to mind.

Possibilities that haunt me in the dark hours and nibble at the edges of my reason. At what stage did Scarsdale become transformed? Or was he, long before the Great Northern Expedition began, already ONE OF THEM?

NEW AND FORTHCOMING TITLES FROM VALANCOURT BOOKS

R. C. Ashby (Ruby Ferguson)	He Arrived at Dusk
Frank Baker	The Birds
Walter Baxter	Look Down in Mercy
Charles Beaumont	The Hunger and Other Stories
David Benedictus	The Fourth of June
Paul Binding	Harmonica's Bridegroom
John Blackburn	A Scent of New-Mown Hay
	Broken Boy
	Blue Octavo
	The Flame and the Wind
	Nothing But the Night
	Bury Him Darkly
	The Household Traitors
	Our Lady of Pain
	The Face of the Lion
	The Cyclops Goblet
	A Beastly Business
Thomas Blackburn	The Feast of the Wolf
John Braine	Room at the Top
	The Vodi
Basil Copper	The Great White Space
	Necropolis
Hunter Davies	Body Charge
Jennifer Dawson	The Ha-Ha
Barry England	Figures in a Landscape
Ronald Fraser	Flower Phantoms
Stephen Gilbert	The Landslide
	Bombardier
	Monkeyface
	The Burnaby Experiments
	Ratman's Notebooks
Martyn Goff	The Plaster Fabric
	The Youngest Director
	Indecent Assault
Stephen Gregory	The Cormorant
Thomas Hinde	Mr. Nicholas
	The Day the Call Came

John Wain	Hurry on Down
	The Smaller Sky
Hugh Walpole	The Killer and the Slain
Keith Waterhouse	There is a Happy Land
	Billy Liar
Colin Wilson	Ritual in the Dark
	Man Without a Shadow
	The World of Violence
	The Philosopher's Stone
	The God of the Labyrinth

Selected Eighteenth and Nineteenth Century Classics

Anonymous	Teleny
	The Sins of the Cities of the Plain
Grant Allen	Miss Cayley's Adventures
Joanna Baillie	Six Gothic Dramas
Eaton Stannard Barrett	The Heroine
William Beckford	Azemia
Mary Elizabeth Braddon	Thou Art the Man
John Buchan	Sir Quixote of the Moors
Hall Caine	The Manxman
Marie Corelli	The Sorrows of Satan
	Ziska
Baron Corvo	Stories Toto Told Me
	Hubert's Arthur
Gabriele D'Annunzio	The Intruder (L'innocente)
Arthur Conan Doyle	Round the Red Lamp
Baron de la Motte Fouqué	The Magic Ring
H. Rider Haggard	Nada the Lily
Sheridan Le Fanu	Carmilla
M. G. Lewis	The Monk
Edward Bulwer Lytton	Eugene Aram
Florence Marryat	The Blood of the Vampire
Richard Marsh	The Beetle
Bertram Mitford	Renshaw Fanning's Quest
John Moore	Zeluco
Ouida	Under Two Flags
Walter Pater	Marius the Epicurean
Bram Stoker	The Lady of the Shroud

CPSIA information can be obtained at www.ICGtesting.com
Printed in the USA
BVOW032243070513

320160BV00002B/9/P